ROBERT BURNS

Robert Burns was born in 1759, the son of a struggling tenant-farmer in Ayrshire, who nevertheless joined with neighbours to employ a university-trained tutor for their children. When very young, Burns read the Bible, the English Augustans and Gray; later he learned some French and a little Latin. The surrounding countryside was rich in folklore, but Scots literature came his way only by chance and it was later in his life that he realized the possibilities of contemporary literature in Scots. Meanwhile the privation and overwork of subsistence farming began the rheumatic heart-disease that was to cause his premature death. His father died bankrupt in 1784 and Burns, as head of the family, leased a farm at Mossgiel. He began to circulate verse satires on Calvinist extremists, and in July 1786 the Church avenged itself by exacting public penance from him and Jean Armour who was pregnant by him and whom he acknowledged as his wife in 1788. *Poems Chiefly in the Scottish Dialect* was published in 1786 and enthusiastically received and Burns spent the winters of 1786–7 and 1787–8 in Edinburgh, acting out with increasing unease the rôle of child of nature and untutored poet of the plough in which the Edinburgh gentry had cast him, seeking relief in the city's hard-drinking low life. An admirer leased him a farm at Ellisland and in 1789 he was appointed to the Excise Division in nearby Dumfries. The farm failed, through lack of capital, and Burns devoted his main energies to the collection and rewriting of Scots songs. He moved to Dumfries in 1791, where, after official investigation into his sympathies for the American and French Revolutions, he was promoted in the Excise and helped to organize local Volunteer units. His health gave way and he died in 1796.

ROBERT BURNS

Selected and edited by

HENRY W. MEIKLE AND

WILLIAM BEATTIE

PENGUIN BOOKS

Penguin Books Ltd, Harmondsworth, Middlesex, England
Viking Penguin Inc., 40 West 23rd Street, New York, New York 10010, U.S.A.
Penguin Books Australia Ltd, Ringwood, Victoria, Australia
Penguin Books Canada Limited, 2801 John Street, Markham, Ontario, Canada L3R 1B4
Penguin Books (N.Z.) Ltd, 182–190 Wairau Road, Auckland 10, New Zealand

—

First published 1946
Reprinted 1947
Revised edition 1953
Reprinted 1958
Reissued 1972
Reprinted 1975
Reprinted with revision 1977
Reprinted 1979, 1981, 1983, 1985, 1986

—

—

Printed and bound in Great Britain by
Cox & Wyman Ltd, Reading
Set in Monotype Bembo

CONTENTS

CONTENTS

CONTENTS

CONTENTS

EDITORS' NOTE 1946

The life of the poet is compiled from condensed quotations from his letters. Unless it is otherwise stated in the list of contents, the text, punctuation, and notes of the poems are taken from the editions published in the poet's lifetime, mainly that of 1793. Most of the songs are taken from James Johnson's The Scots Musical Museum, *vols. 2–6, 1788–1803, and from the texts either in George Thomson's* A Select Collection of Original Scottish Airs, *vols. 2–4, 1798–1805, or in letters received by him from the poet as published by J. Currie in his* The Works of Robert Burns, *vol. 4, 1800.*

ADDITIONAL NOTE 1977

Editorial footnotes are signed EDD. *even where, as in a few instances, they have been written since the death of Dr Meikle in 1958, when the editors had agreed how, within limits set some years before, their work might be bettered.*

LIFE

Born at Alloway, near Ayr, 25 January.   1759

I was born a very poor man's son. My father was gardener
to a worthy gentleman of small estate. Had he continued in
that station, I must have marched off to be one of the little
underlings about a farm-house; but it was his dearest wish
and prayer to have it in his power to keep his children under
his own eye till they could discern between good and evil.

At Mount Oliphant.   1766

So with the assistance of his generous master, my father
ventured on a small farm on his estate.

Though it cost the schoolmaster some thrashings, I made
an excellent English scholar; and by the time I was ten or
eleven years of age, I was a critic in substantives, verbs, and
particles. In my infant and boyish days too, I owed much
to an old woman who resided in the family. She had, I
suppose, the largest collection in the country of tales and
songs concerning devils, ghosts, fairies, brownies, witches,
warlocks, and other trumpery. This cultivated the latent
seeds of poetry.

My father's generous master died; the farm proved a
ruinous bargain; and to clench the misfortune, we fell into
the hands of a factor, who sat for the picture I have drawn
of one in my *Tale of Twa Dogs*. We retrenched our expenses.
We lived very poorly: I was a dextrous ploughman for my
age.

This kind of life – the cheerless gloom of a hermit, with
the unceasing moil of a galley-slave, brought me to my
sixteenth year; a little before which I first committed the
sin of Rhyme. In my fifteenth autumn, my partner [in
harvesting] was a bewitching creature, a year younger than
myself. Among her love-inspiring qualities, she sung

sweetly, and it was her favourite reel to which I attempted giving an embodied vehicle in rhyme. Thus with me began love and poetry.

1777 At Lochlea.

My father entered on a larger farm, about ten miles farther in the country. For four years we lived comfortably here. It is during the time that we lived on this farm that my little story is most eventful.

My reputation for bookish knowledge, a certain wild logical talent, and a strength of thought [made me] generally a welcome guest.

I spent my nineteenth summer on a smuggling coast at a noted school to learn mensuration, surveying, etc., in which I made a pretty good progress, when a charming fillette overset my trigonometry and set me off at a tangent.

I returned home very considerably improved. My reading was enlarged. My life flowed on much in the same course till my twenty-third year. *Vive l'amour et vive la bagatelle* were my sole principles of action.

My twenty-third year was a very important aera. I joined a flax-dresser in a neighbouring town to learn his trade. The shop took fire and I was left like a true poet, not worth a sixpence. From this adventure I learned something of a town life; but the principal thing which gave my mind a turn was a friendship I formed with a young fellow. He was the only man I ever saw who was a greater fool than myself where woman was the presiding star; but he spoke of illicit love with the levity of a sailor, which hitherto I had regarded with horror. Here his friendship did me a mischief.

A difference commencing between my father and his landlord, after three years tossing in the vortex of litigation, my father was just saved from the horrors of a jail by a consumption which, after two years' promises, carried him away.

At Mossgiel, near Mauchline. 1784

When my father died, my brother and I took a neighbouring farm. But the first year from unfortunately buying bad seed, the second from a late harvest, we lost half our crops.

[Then came] a most melancholy affair [Jean Armour] which I cannot yet bear to reflect on. I gave up my part of the farm to my brother and made what little preparation was in my power for Jamaica.

Poems chiefly in the Scottish Dialect printed at Kilmarnock. 1786

Before leaving my native country for ever, I resolved to publish my poems. My vanity was highly gratified by the reception I met with from the public, and besides, I pocketed, all expenses deducted, nearly twenty pounds.

Visits to Edinburgh. 1786–8

I had taken the last farewell of my few friends when a letter from Dr Blacklock to a friend of mine overthrew all my schemes. His opinion that I would meet with encouragement in Edinburgh for a second edition fired me so much that away I posted to that city. At Edinburgh I was in a new world.

By all probability I shall soon be the tenth worthy, and the eighth wise man of the World.

I see the time not distant far when the popular tide shall recede with silent celerity and leave me a barren waste of sand.

1787 Edinburgh Edition of the *Poems*, 'printed for the Author and sold by William Creech'.

I guess I shall clear between two and three hundred pounds by my authorship; with that sum I intend to return to my old acquaintance, the plough, and to commence Farmer.

Tours the Borders and the Highlands.

My journey thro' the Highlands was perfectly inspiring; and I hope I have laid in a new stock of poetical ideas.

Friendship with Mrs M'Lehose – Clarinda.

I determined to cultivate your friendship with the enthusiasm of religion.

I am yours, Clarinda, for life.

1787–96 Contributes Songs to James Johnson's *The Scots Musical Museum*.

An engraver, James Johnson, in Edinburgh, has, not from mercenary views, but from an honest Scotch enthusiasm, set about collecting all our native songs. I have been absolutely crazed about it.

1788 Leases the farm of Ellisland, near Dumfries.

Shortly after my last return to Ayrshire, I married 'my Jean' [Armour].

I do not find my farm that pennyworth I was taught to expect, but I believe, in time, it may be a saving bargain.

1789 Appointed Exciseman.

I know not how the word, exciseman, or still more opprobrious, gauger, will sound in your ears. I too have seen the day when my auditory nerves would have felt very delicately on this subject; but a wife and children are things which have a wonderful power in blunting these kind of sensations. Fifty pounds a year for life, and a provision for widows and orphans, you will allow, is no bad settlement for a poet.

Gives up Ellisland and settles as an Exciseman in Dumfries.   1791

I have sold to my landlord the lease of my farm.
    I have not been so lucky in farming.

Contributes to George Thomson's *A Select Collection*   1792–6
of Original Scottish Airs.

As to any remuneration, you may think my songs either above or below price; for they shall absolutely be the one or the other.

'The Second Edition' of the *Poems*, 'considerably   1793
enlarged', 2 vols., Edinburgh.

A few books which I very much want are all the recompense I crave, together with as many copies of this new edition of my own works as Friendship or Gratitude shall prompt me to present.
    Occasional hard drinking is the devil to me. Taverns I have wholly abandoned: it is the private parties in the family way, among the hard drinking gentlemen of this country, that do me the mischief – but even this I have more than half given over.

'A new Edition considerably enlarged' of the *Poems*.   1794
Similar to that of 1793.

1795 **The Excise.**

I am on the supervisors' list, and in two or three years I shall be at the head of that list. The moment I am appointed supervisor I may be nominated on the collectors' list. A collectorship varies much from better than two hundred a year to near a thousand. They have, besides a handsome income, a life of compleat leisure. A life of literary leisure, with a decent competence, is the summit of my wishes.

1796 **Last Illness.**

I fear the voice of the bard will soon be heard among you no more! For these eight or ten months I have been ailing, sometimes bedfast and sometimes not; but these last three months I have been tortured with an excruciating rheumatism which has reduced me to nearly the last stage.

Died at Dumfries, 21 July.

LIST OF COMMON WORDS

a', all
aboon, above
ae, a, one
aff, off
aft, oft
ain, own
amaist, almost
an, if
ance, once
ane, one
auld, old
ava, at all, of all
awa', away
ay, aye, always
ayont, beyond

baith, both
banes, bones
bauld, bold
bonie, bony, pretty, fine
braid, broad
braw, fine

ca', call, drive
cauld, cold

daur, dare
dinna, don't

e'e, eye
e'en, eyes

fa', fall
fou, full, drunk
frae, from

gae, go
gaed, went
gaung, going
gie, give
gif, if
gin, if
gude, guid, good

hae, have

ilk, ilka, each, every
ither, other

ken, know

mair, more
maist, almost
maun, must
monie, many

na, nae, no
nane, none
niest, next

onie, ony, any
out-owre, away over
ower, over, too

List of Common Words

sae, so

saft, soft

sair, sore, hard

sic, such

simmer, summer

stane, stone

syne, then

ta'en, taken

thae, those

twa, two

unco, uncommonly, very

wad, would

wha, who

whyles, sometimes

yon, that

yont, beyond

Poems in the Kilmarnock Edition, 1786

THE TWA DOGS

A Tale

'Twas in that place o' Scotland's isle,
That bears the name o' Auld King Coil,[1]
Upon a bonie day in June,
When wearing thro' the afternoon,
Twa dogs, that were na thrang at hame,   busy
Forgather'd ance upon a time.   Met

The first I'll name, they ca'd him Cæsar,
Was keepit for his Honor's pleasure;
His hair, his size, his mouth, his lugs,   ears
Shew'd he was nane o' Scotland's dogs,
But whalpit some place far abroad,
Whare sailors gang to fish for Cod.

His locked, letter'd, braw brass collar   handsome
Shew'd him the gentleman and scholar;
But tho' he was o' high degree,
The fient a pride, na pride had he,   devil
But wad hae spent an hour caressin,
Ev'n wi' a tinkler-gypsey's messin: mongrel, cur
At kirk or market, mill or smiddie,   smithy
Nae tawted tyke, tho' e'er sae duddie,   matted cur; ragged
But he wad stan't, as glad to see him,   would have stood
And stroan't on stanes an' hillocks wi' him.   watered

The tither was a ploughman's collie,   The other
A rhyming, ranting, raving billie,   rollicking; young fellow
Wha for his friend and comrade had him,

1. Kyle in Ayrshire. – EDD.

21

And in his freaks had Luath ca'd him,
After some dog in Highland sang,[1]
long ago   Was made lang syne, Lord knows how lang.

wise   He was a gash an' faithful tyke,
leapt; ditch; wall   As ever lap a sheugh or dyke.
pleasant,
white-
striped   His honest, sonsie, baws'nt face
every   Ay gat him friends in ilka place;
shaggy   His breast was white, his touzie back
Weel clad wi' coat o' glossy black;
ample   His gawcie tail, wi' upward curl,
buttocks   Hung owre his hurdies wi' a swirl.

fond of each
other   Nae doubt but they were fain o' ither,
very intimate   An' unco pack an' thick thegither;
sometimes;
scented   Wi' social nose whyles snuff'd an' snowkit,
moles;
dug up   Whyles mice an' moudieworts they howkit;
Whyles scour'd awa in lang excursion,
An' worry'd ither in diversion;
Till tir'd at last wi' mony a farce,
They sat them down upon their arse,
And there began a lang digression
About the *lords o' the creation*.

CÆSAR

I've aften wonder'd, honest Luath,
What sort o' life poor dogs like you have;
An' when the gentry's life I saw,
at all   What way poor bodies liv'd ava.

1. Cuchullin's dog in Ossian's Fingal.

Our Laird gets in his racked rents,
His coals, his kain, and a' his stents: *rents in kind; dues*
He rises when he likes himsel;
His flunkies answer at the bell;
He ca's his coach; he ca's his horse;
He draws a bonie, silken purse
As lang's my tail, whare thro the steeks,   *stitches*
The yellow letter'd Geordie keeks.   *guinea peeps*

Frae morn to e'en it's nought but toiling,
At baking, roasting, frying, boiling;
An' tho' the gentry first are stechin,   *stuffing*
Yet ev'n the ha' folk fill their pechan   *servants; stomach*
Wi' sauce, ragouts, and siclike trashtrie,
That's little short o' downright wastrie.
Our Whipper-in, wee, blastit wonner,   *wonder*
Poor, worthless elf, it eats a dinner,
Better than ony tenant man
His Honour has in a' the lan':
An' what poor cot-folk pit their painch in,   *put; paunch*
I own it's past my comprehension.

LUATH

Trowth, Cæsar, whyles they're fash't enough;   *bothered*
A cotter howkin in a sheugh,   *digging*
Wi' dirty stanes biggin a dyke,   *building*
Baring a quarry, and siclike,   *Clearing*
Himsel, a wife, he thus sustains,
A smytrie o' wee duddie weans,   *swarm; little ragged children*
An' nought but his han' darg to keep   *hands' labour*
Them right an' tight in thack an' rape.   *thatch and rope*

An' when they meet wi' sair disasters,
Like loss o' health or want o' masters,

Ye maist wad think, a wee touch langer,
An' they maun starve o' cauld and hunger:
But how it comes, I never kend yet,
They're maistly wonderfu' contented;

stout lads;
young
women

An' buirdly chiels, an' clever hizzies,
Are bred in sic a way as this is.

CÆSAR

But then to see how ye're negleckit,
How huff'd, and cuff'd, and disrespeckit!
Lord, man, our gentry care as little
For delvers, ditchers, an' sic cattle;
They gang as saucy by poor folk,

badger

As I wad by a stinking brock.

rent-

I've notic'd, on our Laird's court-day,

sad

An' mony a time my heart's been wae,
Poor tenant bodies, scant o' cash,

endure;
abuse

How they maun thole a factor's snash;
He'll stamp an' threaten, curse an' swear,

seize

He'll apprehend them, poind their gear:
While they maun stan', wi' aspect humble,
An' hear it a', an' fear an' tremble!

I see how folk live that hae riches;
But surely poor folk maun be wretches!

LUATH

They're nae sae wretched's ane wad think;

poverty's

Tho' constantly on poortith's brink,
They're sae accustom'd wi' the sight,
The view o't gies them little fright.

The Twa Dogs

Then chance an' fortune are sae guided,
They're ay in less or mair provided;
An' tho' fatigu'd wi' close employment,
A blink o' rest's a sweet enjoyment.   moment

The dearest comfort o' their lives,
Their grushie weans an' faithfu' wives;   thriving
The prattling things are just their pride,
That sweetens a' their fire-side.

An' whyles twalpennie worth o' nappy   ale
Can mak the bodies unco happy;
They lay aside their private cares,
To mind the Kirk and State affairs;
They'll talk o' patronage and priests,
Wi' kindling fury in their breasts,
Or tell what new taxation's comin,
An' ferlie at the folk in Lon'on.   marvel

As bleak-fac'd Hallowmass returns,
They get the jovial, ranting Kirns,   harvest-
When rural life, o' ev'ry station,   homes
Unite in common recreation;
Love blinks, Wit slaps, an' social Mirth   glances
Forgets there's Care upo' the earth.

That merry day the year begins,
They bar the door on frosty win's;
The nappy reeks wi' mantling ream,   smokes;
An' sheds a heart-inspiring steam;   froth
The luntin pipe, an' sneeshin mill,   smoking;
Are handed round wi' right guid will;   snuff-box
The cantie, auld folks, crackin crouse,   cheery;
                                                        talking

25

merrily
romping

The young anes ranting thro' the house —
My heart has been sae fain to see them,
That I for joy hae barkit wi' them.

Still it's owre true that ye hae said,
too often   Sic game is now owre aften play'd;
There's monie a creditable stock
seemly   O' decent, honest fawsont folk,
Are riven out baith root and branch,
Some rascal's pridefu' greed to quench,
Wha thinks to knit himsel the faster
In favor wi' some gentle Master,
perhaps busy   Wha ablins thrang a parliamentin
For Britain's guid his saul indentin —

CÆSAR

Faith   Haith, lad, ye little ken about it;
For Britain's guid! guid faith! I doubt it.
going   Say rather, gaun as Premiers lead him,
An' saying *aye* or *no*'s they bid him:
At operas an' plays parading,
Mortgaging, gambling, masquerading:
Or maybe, in a frolic daft,
To Hague or Calais taks a waft,
To mak a tour, an' tak a whirl,
To learn *bon ton* an' see the worl'.

There, at Vienna or Versailles,
He rives his father's auld entails;
Or by Madrid he taks the rout,
fight; cattle   To thrum guitars an' fecht wi' nowt;

Or down Italian vista startles,
Whore hunting amang groves o' myrtles:
Then bouses drumly German water,   muddy
To mak himsel look fair and fatter,
An' clear the consequential sorrows,
Love-gifts of Carnival Signoras.[1]

For Britain's guid! for her destruction!
Wi' dissipation, feud an' faction.

LUATH

Hech man! dear sirs! is that the gate   way
They waste sae mony a braw estate!
Are we sae foughten an' harass'd   worn out
For gear to gang that gate at last!   wealth to go

O would they stay aback frae courts,
An' please themsels wi' countra sports,
It wad for ev'ry ane be better,
The Laird, the Tenant, an' the Cotter!
For thae frank, rantin, ramblin billies,   those; roistering
Fient haet o' them's ill hearted fellows;   Devil a one
Except for breakin o' their timmer,   timber
Or speakin lightly o' their Limmer,   Mistress
Or shootin o' a hare or moorcock,
The ne'er-a-bit they're ill to poor folk.

But will ye tell me, master Cæsar,
Sure great folk's life's a life o' pleasure?
Nae cauld nor hunger e'er can steer them,   disturb
The vera thought o't need na fear them.

1. See note on p.29. – EDD.

CÆSAR

Lord, man, were ye but whyles whare I am,
The gentles ye wad ne'er envy 'em.

It's true, they need na starve or sweat,
Thro' winter's cauld, or Simmer's heat;

hard They've nae sair wark to craze their banes,
gripes and An' fill auld age wi' grips an' granes;
groans But human bodies are sic fools,
For a' their colleges and schools,
That when nae real ills perplex them,
They mak enow themsels to vex them;

annoy An' ay the less they hae to sturt them,
In like proportion, less will hurt them.
A country fellow at the pleugh,
His acre's till'd, he's right eneugh;
A country girl at her wheel,

dozen Her dizzen's done, she's unco weel:
But Gentlemen, an' Ladies warst,

utter Wi' ev'n down want o' wark are curst.
They loiter, lounging, lank, an' lazy;

devil a thing Tho' deil haet ails them, yet uneasy;
Their days, insipid, dull an' tasteless,
Their nights, unquiet, lang, and restless,
An' ev'n their sports, their balls an' races,
Their galloping thro' public places,
There's sic parade, sic pomp an' art,
The joy can scarcely reach the heart.
The Men cast out in party matches,

solder Then sowther a' in deep debauches,
Ae night, they're mad wi' drink an' whoring,
Niest day their life is past enduring.
The Ladies arm-in-arm in clusters,

The Twa Dogs

As great an' gracious a' as sisters;
But hear their absent thoughts o' ither,
They're a' run deils an' jads thegither.   *downright*
Whyles, owre the wee bit cup an' platie,
They sip the scandal potion pretty;
Or lee-lang nights, wi' crabbit leuks,   *live-long*
Pore owre the devil's pictur'd beuks;   *playing-cards*
Stake on a chance a farmer's stackyard,
An' cheat like ony unhang'd blackguard.

    There's some exception, man an' woman;
But this is Gentry's life in common.

    By this, the sun was out o' sight,
An' darker gloamin brought the night:
The bum-clock humm'd wi' lazy drone,   *beetle*
The kye stood rowtin i' the loan;   *cattle; lowing; pasture*
When up they gat an' shook their lugs,
Rejoic'd they were na *men*, but *dogs*;
An' each took aff his several way,
Resolv'd to meet some ither day.

1. In the 1st edn. (1786) the reading on p.27 is
        An' purge the bitter ga's an' cankers
        O'curst Venetian b—res an' ch—ncres.

ga' = gall   bore = crack   chancre = ulcer

SCOTCH DRINK

Gie him strong drink until he wink,
That's sinking in despair;
An' liquor guid to fire his bluid,
That's prest wi' grief an' care:
There let him bouse, an' deep carouse,
Wi' bumpers flowing o'er,
Till he forgets his loves or debts,
An' minds his griefs no more.

SOLOMON'S PROVERBS, xxxi. 6, 7

Let other Poets raise a fracas
'Bout vines, an' wines, an' druken Bacchus,
torment An' crabbit names an' stories wrack us,
ear An' grate our lug,
barley I sing the juice Scotch bear can mak us,
In glass or jug.

O thou, my Muse! guid, auld Scotch Drink!
winding;
dodge Whether thro' wimplin worms thou jink,
cream Or, richly brown, ream owre the brink,
foam In glorious faem,
Inspire me, till I lisp and wink,
To sing thy name!

meadows Let husky Wheat the haughs adorn,
oats; bearded An' Aits set up their awnie horn,
An' Pease and Beans, at een or morn,
Perfume the plain,
Lief is me Leeze me on thee, John Barleycorn,
Thou king o' grain!

chews her
cud On thee aft Scotland chows her cood,
pliable; pick In souple scones, the wale o' food!

30

Scotch Drink

Or tumbling in the boiling flood
         Wi' kail an' beef;   *greens*
But when thou pours thy strong heart's blood,
         There thou shines chief.

Food fills the wame, an' keeps us livin;   *belly*
Tho' life's a gift no worth receivin,
When heavy-dragg'd wi' pine an' grievin;
         But oil'd by thee,
The wheels o' life gae down-hill, scrievin,   *go; careering*
         Wi' rattlin glee.

Thou clears the head o' doited Lear;   *stupid Learning*
Thou chears the heart o' drooping Care;
Thou strings the nerves o' Labor sair,
         At's weary toil;
Thou ev'n brightens dark Despair
         Wi' gloomy smile.

Aft, clad in massy, siller weed,   *silver dress*
Wi' Gentles thou erects thy head;
Yet humbly kind, in time o' need,
         The poor man's wine;
His wee drap parritch, or his bread,   *porridge*
         Thou kitchens fine.   *seasons*

Thou art the life o' public haunts;
But thee, what were our fairs and rants?   *Without; sprees*
Ev'n godly meetings o' the saunts,
         By thee inspir'd,
When gaping they besiege the tents,
         Are doubly fir'd.

Scotch Drink

That merry night we get the corn in,
O sweetly, then, thou reams the horn in!
Or reekin on a New-year mornin
        In cog or bicker,
An' just a wee drap sp'ritual burn in,
        An' gusty sucker!

When Vulcan gies his bellows breath,
An' ploughmen gather wi' their graith,
O rare! to see thee fizz an' freath
        I' th' lugget caup!
Then Burnewin comes on like Death
        At ev'ry chap.

Nae mercy, then, for airn or steel;
The brawnie, bainie, ploughman chiel
Brings hard owrehip, wi' sturdy wheel,
        The strong forehammer,
Till block an' studdie ring an' reel
        Wi' dinsome clamour.

When skirlin weanies see the light,
Thou maks the gossips clatter bright,
How fumbling Cuifs their Dearies slight,
        Wae worth the name!
Nae Howdie gets a social night,
        Or plack frae them.

When neebors anger at a plea,
An' just as wud as wud can be,
How easy can the barley-brie
        Cement the quarrel!
It's aye the cheapest Lawyer's fee
        To taste the barrel.

Scotch Drink

Alake! that e'er my Muse has reason
To wyte her countrymen wi' treason!   *charge*
But monie daily weet their weason   *wet;*
      Wi' liquors nice,   *weasand*
An' hardly, in a winter season,
      E'er spier her price.   *ask*

Wae worth that brandy, burning trash!
Fell source o' monie a pain an' brash!   *illness*
Twins monie a poor, doylt, druken hash   *robs; stupid, drunken oaf*
      O' half his days;
An' sends beside, auld Scotland's cash
      To her warst faes.   *foes*

Ye Scots, wha wish auld Scotland well,
Ye chief, to you my tale I tell,
Poor, plackless devils like mysel,   *penniless*
      It sets you ill,   *becomes*
Wi' bitter, dearthfu' wines to mell,   *meddle*
      Or foreign gill.

May gravels round his blather wrench,   *bladder*
An' gouts torment him, inch by inch,
Wha twists his gruntle wi' a glunch   *face; frown*
      O' sour disdain,
Out owre a glass o' whisky punch
      Wi' honest men!

O Whisky! soul o' plays an' pranks!
Accept a Bardie's gratefu' thanks!
When wanting thee, what tuneless cranks
      Are my poor Verses!
Thou comes — they rattle i' their ranks
      At ither's arses!

Scotch Drink

Thee Ferintosh! O sadly lost!
Scotland lament frae coast to coast!
cough   Now colic-grips, an' barkin hoast,
        May kill us a';
For loyal Forbes' charter'd boast
        Is ta'en awa![1]

Those   Thae curst horse-leeches o' th' Excise,
stills   Wha mak the Whisky stells their prize!
Haud up thy han' Deil! ance, twice, thrice!
spies   There, seize the blinkers!
brimstone   An' bake them up in brunstane pies
        For poor damn'd drinkers.

Fortune! if thou'll but gie me still
Whole   Hale breeks, a scone, an' whisky gill,
breeks
abundance   An' rowth o' rhyme to rave at will,
        Tak a' the rest,
An' deal't about as thy blind skill
        Directs thee best.

---

1. Duncan Forbes of Culloden had a concession to distil whisky at
Ferintosh. It was withdrawn in 1785. The name is pronounced in
two syllables, 'Forbès'. – EDD.

THE HOLY FAIR[1]

A robe of seeming truth and trust
Hid crafty Observation;
And secret hung, with poison'd crust,
The dirk of Defamation:
A mask that like the gorge show'd,
Dye-varying on the pigeon;
And for a mantle large and broad,
He wrapt him in Religion.

HYPOCRISY A-LA-MODE

I

Upon a simmer Sunday morn,
   When Nature's face is fair,
I walked forth to view the corn,
   An' snuff the caller air.   *fresh*
The rising sun, owre Galston muirs,
   Wi' glorious light was glintin;
The hares were hirplin down the furs,   *hopping; furrows*
   The lav'rocks they were chantin   *larks*
                Fu' sweet that day.

II

As lightsomely I glowr'd abroad,   *gazed*
   To see a scene sae gay,
Three Hizzies, early at the road,   *young women*
   Cam skelpin up the way.   *spanking*
Twa had manteeles o' dolefu' black,
   But ane wi' lyart lining;   *grey*
The third, that gaed a wee a-back,   *walked a bit behind*
   Was in the fashion shining
                Fu' gay that day.

1. Holy Fair is a common phrase in the West of Scotland for a sacramental occasion.

III

The twa appear'd like sisters twin,
  In feature, form, an' claes;
clothes

Their visage wither'd, lang an' thin,
  An' sour as ony slaes:
sloes

The third cam up, hap-step-an'-lowp,
hop; jump
  As light as ony lambie,

An' wi' a curchie low did stoop,
curtsey
  As soon as e'er she saw me,
      Fu' kind that day.

IV

Wi' bonnet aff, quoth I, 'Sweet lass,
  'I think ye seem to ken me;
'I'm sure I've seen that bonie face,
  'But yet I canna name ye.'
Quo' she, an' laughin as she spak,
  An' taks me by the hauns,
bulk
'Ye, for my sake, hae gi'en the feck
  'Of a' the ten commauns
rip
      'A screed some day.

V

'My name is Fun – your cronie dear,
  'The nearest friend ye hae;
'An' this is Superstition here,
  'An' that's Hypocrisy.
going
'I'm gaun to Mauchline Holy Fair,
merry-making
  'To spend an hour in daffin:
If; wrinkled
'Gin ye'll go there, yon runkl'd pair,
  'We will get famous laughin
      'At them this day.'

VI

Quoth I, 'With a' my heart, I'll do't;
   'I'll get my Sunday's sark on,   shirt
'An' meet you on the holy spot;
   'Faith, we'se hae fine remarkin!'   we'll
Then I gaed hame at crowdie-time,   went;
   An' soon I made me ready;   porridge-
For roads were clad, frae side to side,
   Wi' monie a wearie body,
          In droves that day.

VII

Here, farmers gash, in ridin graith,   shrewd;
   Gaed hoddin by their cotters;   attire
There, swankies young, in braw braid-claith, jogging
   Are springin owre the gutters.   strapping
The lasses, skelpin barefit, thrang,   fellows
   In silks an' scarlets glitter;   walking
Wi' sweet-milk cheese, in monie a whang, smartly;
   An' farls, bak'd wi' butter,   thronging
         Fu' crump that day.   large slice

                                       oatcakes

                                       crisp

VIII

When by the plate we set our nose,
   Weel heaped up wi' ha'pence,
A greedy glowr Black Bonnet throws,   stare; Elder
   An' we maun draw our tippence.
Then in we go to see the show,
   On ev'ry side they're gath'rin;
Some carryin dails, some chairs an' stools, planks
   An' some are busy bleth'rin   talking
         Right loud that day.

IX

Here stands a shed to fend the show'rs,
    An' screen our countra Gentry,
There, racer Jess, an' twa-three whores, *[two or three]*
    Are blinkin at the entry. *[leering]*
Here sits a raw o' tittlin jads, *[whispering / jades]*
    Wi' heaving breast an' bare neck;
An' there, a batch o' wabster lads, *[weaver]*
    Blackguarding frae Kilmarnock
            For fun this day.

X

Here some are thinkin on their sins,
    An' some upo' their claes; *[clothes]*
Ane curses feet that fyl'd his shins, *[soiled]*
    Anither sighs an' prays:
On this hand sits a chosen swatch, *[sample]*
    Wi' screw'd-up, grace-proud faces;
On that, a set o' Chaps, at watch,
    Thrang winkin on the lasses *[Busy]*
            To chairs that day.

XI

O happy is that man an' blest!
    Nae wonder that it pride him!
Wha's ain dear lass, that he likes best,
    Comes clinkin down beside him!
Wi' arm repos'd on the chair-back,
    He sweetly does compose him;
Which, by degrees, slips round her neck,
    An's loof upon her bosom *[palm]*
            Unkend that day.

XII

Now a' the congregation o'er
   Is silent expectation;
For Moodie speels the holy door,   climbs
   Wi' tidings o' damnation.
Should Hornie, as in ancient days,   the Devil
   'Mang sons o' God present him,
The vera sight o' Moodie's face,
   To's ain het hame had sent him   hot
             Wi' fright that day.

XIII

Hear how he clears the points o' faith
   Wi' rattlin an' thumpin!
Now meekly calm, now wild in wrath,
   He's stampin, an' he's jumpin!
His lengthen'd chin, his turn'd-up snout,
   His eldritch squeel an' gestures,   unearthly
O how they fire the heart devout,
   Like cantharidian plasters,
             On sic a day!

XIV

But hark! the tent has chang'd its voice;
   There's peace an' rest nae langer:
For a' the real judges rise,
   They canna sit for anger.
Smith opens out his cauld harangues,
   On practice and on morals;
An' aff the godly pour in thrangs,
   To gie the jars an' barrels
             A lift that day.

XV

What signifies his barren shine,
  Of moral pow'rs an' reason?
His English style, an' gesture fine,
  Are a' clean out o' season.
Like Socrates or Antonine,
  Or some auld pagan Heathen,
The moral man he does define,
  But ne'er a word o' faith in
        That's right that day.

XVI

In guid time comes an antidote
  Against sic poison'd nostrum;
-foot   For Peebles, frae the water-fit,
  Ascends the holy rostrum:
See, up he's got the word o' God,
prim   An' meek an' mim has view'd it,
While Common-Sense has taen the road,
  An' aff, an' up the Cowgate
        Fast, fast that day.

XVII

next   Wee Miller niest, the Guard relieves,
gabbles   An' Orthodoxy raibles,
Tho' in his heart he weel believes,
  An' thinks it auld wives' fables:
fellow; living   But faith! the birkie wants a Manse,
artfully;
humbugs   So, cannilie he hums them;
Altho' his carnal wit an' sense
Nearly half-   Like hafflins-wise o'ercomes him
        At times that day.

XVIII

Now, butt an' ben[1] the Change-house fills,   tavern
   Wi' yill-caup Commentators: ale-cup
Here's crying out for bakes an' gills,   biscuits
   An' there the pint-stowp clatters;
While thick an' thrang, an' loud an' lang,
   Wi' Logic, an' wi' Scripture,
They raise a din, that, in the end,
   Is like to breed a rupture
          O' wrath that day.

XIX

Leeze me on Drink! it gies us mair   Lief is me
   Than either School or Colledge:
It kindles Wit, it waukens Lair,   wakens
          learning
   It pangs us fou o' Knowledge.   crams
Be't whisky gill or penny wheep,   small beer
   Or ony stronger potion,
It never fails, on drinkin deep,
   To kittle up our notion,   tickle
          By night or day.

XX

The lads an' lasses, blythely bent
   To mind baith saul an' body,
Sit round the table, weel content,
   An' steer about the toddy.
On this ane's dress, an' that ane's leuk,
   They're makin observations;
While some are cozie i' the neuk,   corner
   An' formin assignations
          To meet some day.

1. The country kitchen and parlour. – BURNS'S GLOSSARY.

XXI

But now the Lord's ain trumpet touts,   *sounds*
   Till a' the hills are rairin,   *roaring*
An' echos back return the shouts;
   Black Russell is na spairin:
His piercing words, like Highlan swords,
   Divide the joints an' marrow;
His talk o' Hell, whare devils dwell,
   Our vera 'Sauls does harrow'[1]
         Wi' fright that day!

XXII

A vast, unbottom'd, boundless pit,
   Fill'd fou o' lowin brunstane,   *full; flaming brimstone*
Wha's ragin flame, an' scorchin heat,
   Wad melt the hardest whun-stane!   *whin-stone*
The half asleep start up wi' fear,
   An' think they hear it roarin,
When presently it does appear,
   'Twas but some neebor snorin
         Asleep that day.

XXIII

'Twad be owre lang a tale to tell,
   How monie stories past,
An' how they crouded to the yill,   *ale*
   When they were a' dismist:
How drink gaed round, in cogs an' caups,   *wooden cups*
   Amang the furms an' benches;   *forms*
An' cheese an' bread, frae women's laps,
   Was dealt about in lunches,   *large pieces*
         An' dawds that day.   *lumps*

1. Shakespeare's Hamlet.

XXIV

In comes a gaucie, gash Guidwife,   jolly, shrewd
 An' sits down by the fire;
Syne draws her kebbuck an' her knife,   Then; cheese
 The lasses they are shyer.
The auld Guidmen, about the grace,
 Frae side to side they bother,
Till some ane by his bonnet lays,   aside
 An' gies them't, like a tether,   rope
     Fu' lang that day.

XXV

Waesucks! for him that gets nae lass,   Alas!
 Or lasses that hae naething!
Sma' need has he to say a grace,
 Or melvie his braw claithing!   soil with
              meal
O Wives be mindfu', ance yoursel
 How bonie lads ye wanted,
An' dinna, for a kebbuck-heel,
 Let lasses be affronted
    On sic a day!

XXVI

Now Clinkumbell, wi' rattlin tow,   Bellringer;
              rope
 Begins to jow an' croon;   ring and
              sound
Some swagger hame, the best they dow, can
 Some wait the afternoon.
At slaps the billies halt a blink,   gaps;
              fellows; bit
 Till lasses strip their shoon: take off
Wi' faith an' hope, an' love an' drink,
 They're a' in famous tune
    For crack that day.   talk

XXVII

How monie hearts this day converts
  O' Sinners and o' Lasses!
Their hearts o' stane gin night are gane,
  As saft as ony flesh is.
There's some are fou o' love divine;
  There's some are fou o' brandy;
An' monie jobs that day begin,
  May end in Houghmagandie
        Some ither day.

by nightfall; gone

fornication

ADDRESS TO THE DEIL

O Prince! O Chief of many throned Pow'rs,
That led th' embattl'd Seraphim to war –
                                    MILTON

O Thou! whatever title suit thee,
Auld Hornie, Satan, Nick, or Clootie,   *Cloven-Foot*
Wha in yon cavern grim an' sootie,
        Clos'd under hatches,
Spairges about the brunstane cootie,   *Splashes;*
                                               brimstone
                                               bowl
        To scaud poor wretches!   *scald*

Hear me, auld Hangie, for a wee,   *Hangman*
An' let poor, damned bodies be;
I'm sure sma' pleasure it can gie,
        Ev'n to a deil,
To skelp an' scaud poor dogs like me,   *slap*
        An' hear us squeel!

Great is thy pow'r, an' great thy fame;
Far kend an' noted is thy name;
An' tho' yon lowin heugh's thy hame,   *flaming pit*
        Thou travels far;
An' faith! thou's neither lag nor lame,   *backward*
        Nor blate nor scaur.   *bashful;*
                                               scared

Whyles, ranging like a roarin lion,   *Now*
For prey, a' holes an' corners tryin;
Whyles, on the strong-wing'd Tempest flyin,
        Tirlin the kirks;   *Unroofing*
Whyles, in the human bosom pryin,
        Unseen thou lurks.

Address to the Deil

I've heard my reverend Graunie say,
In lanely glens ye like to stray;
Or where auld, ruin'd castles, gray,
      Nod to the moon,
Ye fright the nightly wand'rer's way,
      Wi' eldritch croon.

When twilight did my Graunie summon,
_{decent} To say her pray'rs, douce, honest woman!
_{beyond} Aft yont the dyke she's heard you bummin,
      Wi' eerie drone;
_{elder-trees} Or, rustlin, thro' the boortries comin,
      Wi' heavy groan.

Ae dreary, windy, winter night,
_{slanting} The stars shot down wi' sklentin light,
Wi' you, mysel, I gat a fright,
      Ayont the lough;
Ye, like a rash-buss, stood in sight,
      Wi' waving sugh.

_{fist} The cudgel in my nieve did shake,
Each bristl'd hair stood like a stake,
_{hoarse} When wi' an eldritch, stoor quaick, quaick,
      Amang the springs,
_{fluttered} Awa ye squatter'd like a drake,
      On whistling wings.

Let warlocks grim, an' wither'd hags,
_{ragwort} Tell how wi' you on ragweed nags,
They skim the muirs an' dizzy crags,
      Wi' wicked speed;
And in kirk-yards renew their leagues,
_{dug up}   Owre howkit dead.

Address to the Deil

Thence, countra wives, wi' toil an' pain,   country
May plunge an' plunge the kirn in vain;   churn
For, Oh! the yellow treasure's taen
      By witching skill;
An' dawtit, twal-pint Hawkie's gaen   petted / twelve-pint / cow's gone
      As yell's the Bill.   dry as; bull

Thence, mystic knots mak great abuse,
On young Guidmen, fond, keen, an' crouse;   husbands; confident
When the best wark-lume i' the house,   tool
      By cantraip wit,   magic
Is instant made no worth a louse,
      Just at the bit.   when needed

When thowes dissolve the snawy hoord,   thaws; hoard
An' float the jinglin icy-boord,   -surface
Then, Water-kelpies haunt the foord,
      By your direction,
An' nighted Trav'llers are allur'd
      To their destruction.

An' aft your moss-traversing Spunkies   bog-; will-o'-the-wisps
Decoy the wight that late an' drunk is:
The bleezin, curst, mischievous monkies
      Delude his eyes,
Till in some miry slough he sunk is,
      Ne'er mair to rise.

When Masons' mystic word an' grip,
In storms an' tempests raise you up,
Some cock or cat your rage maun stop,   must
      Or, strange to tell!
The youngest Brother ye wad whip
      Aff straught to hell.   straight

Lang syne in Eden's bonie yard,
When youthfu' lovers first were pair'd,
An' all the Soul of Love they shar'd,
   The raptur'd hour,
Sweet on the fragrant, flow'ry swaird,
   In shady bow'r:

Long ago;
garden

Then you, ye auld, snick-drawing dog!
Ye cam to Paradise incog.
An' play'd on man a cursed brogue,
   (Black be your fa'!)
An' gied the infant warld a shog,
   'Maist ruin'd a'.

stealthy
(latch-drawing)

trick

shake
Almost

D'ye mind that day, when in a bizz,
Wi' reekit duds, an' reestit gizz,
Ye did present your smoutie phiz,
   'Mang better folk,
An' sklented on the man of Uzz
   Your spitefu' joke?

bustle
smoky;
scorched wig
smutty

cast

An' how ye gat him i' your thrall,
An' brak him out o' house an' hal',
While scabs an' botches did him gall,
   Wi' bitter claw,
An' lows'd his ill-tongu'd, wicked Scawl,
   Was warst ava?

loosed; scold

of all

But a' your doings to rehearse,
Your wily snares an' fechtin fierce,
Sin' that day Michael[1] did you pierce,
   Down to this time,
Wad ding a Lallan tongue, or Erse,
   In prose or rhyme.

fighting

beat; Low-
land

1. *Vide* Milton, Book V.

Address to the Deil

An' now, auld Cloots, I ken ye're thinkin,
A certain Bardie's rantin, drinkin,   roistering
Some luckless hour will send him linkin   hurrying
       To your black pit;
But, faith! he'll turn a corner jinkin,   dodging
       An' cheat you yet.

But fare you weel, auld Nickie-ben!
O wad ye tak a thought an' men'!
Ye aiblins might – I dinna ken –   perhaps
       Still hae a stake –
I'm wae to think upo' yon den,   woe
       Ev'n for your sake!

THE DEATH AND DYING WORDS OF POOR MAILIE,

THE AUTHOR'S ONLY PET YOWE:
AN UNCO MOURNFU' TALE

Mollie

ewe

As Mailie, an' her lambs thegither, — together
Was ae day nibbling on the tether,
Upon her cloot she coost a hitch, — hoof; cast
An' owre she warsl'd in the ditch: — wrestled
There, groaning, dying, she did lie,
When Hughoc[1] he cam doytin by. — Hugh; doddering

Wi' glowrin een, an' lifted han's, — staring
Poor Hughoc like a statue stan's;
He saw her days were near hand ended,
But, waes my heart! he could na mend it! — woe is
He gaped wide, but naething spak;
At length poor Mailie silence brak.

'O thou, whase lamentable face
Appears to mourn my woefu' case!
My dying words attentive hear,
An' bear them to my Master dear.

'Tell him, if e'er again he keep
As muckle gear as buy a sheep, — much money
O, bid him never tie them mair
Wi' wicked strings o' hemp or hair!
But ca' them out to park or hill, — drive
An' let them wander at their will:
So may his flock increase, an' grow
To scores o' lambs, an' packs o' woo'!

1. A neibor herd-callan [shepherd-lad].

50

'Tell him, he was a Master kin',
An' ay was guid to me an' mine;
An' now my dying charge I gie him,
My helpless lambs, I trust them wi' him.

'O, bid him save their harmless lives,
Frae dogs, an' tods, an' butchers knives!   foxes
But gie them guid cow-milk their fill,
Till they be fit to fend themsel;
An' tent them duly, e'en an' morn,   tend
Wi' teats o' hay an' ripps o' corn.   small quan-
                                                tities;
                                                handfuls

'An' may they never learn the gaets   ways
Of ither vile, wanrestfu' pets!   restless
To slink thro' slaps, an' reave an' steal,   gaps
At stacks o' pease, or stocks o' kail.   greens
So may they, like their great Forbears,   ancestors
For monie a year come thro' the sheers:
So wives will gie them bits o' bread,
An' bairns greet for them when they're dead.   weep

'My poor toop-lamb, my son an' heir,   tup-
O, bid him breed him up wi' care!
An' if he live to be a beast,
To pit some havins in his breast!   manners
An' warn him, what I winna name,   will not
To stay content wi' yowes at hame;
An' no to rin an' wear his cloots,
Like other menseless, graceless brutes.   unmannerly

'An' niest, my yowie, silly thing,   little ewe,
                                                helpless
Gude keep thee frae a tether string!
O, may thou ne'er forgather up   make friends

51

Dying Words of Poor Mailie

Wi' onie blastit, moorland toop;
keep company   But ay keep mind to moop an' mell,
Wi' sheep o' credit like thysel!

'And now, my bairns, wi' my last breath,
I lea'e my blessin wi' you baith:
An' when you think upo' your Mither,
Remember   Mind to be kind to ane anither.

'Now, honest Hughoc, dinna fail
To tell my Master a' my tale;
An' bid him burn this cursed tether,
bladder   An', for thy pains thou'se get my blather.'

This said, poor Mailie turn'd her head,
eyes   An' clos'd her een amang the dead!

POOR MAILIE'S ELEGY

Lament in rhyme, lament in prose,
Wi' saut tears trickling down your nose;   *salt*
Our Bardie's fate is at a close,
        Past a' remead;   *remedy*
The last, sad cape-stane of his woes;   *cope-stone*
        Poor Mailie's dead!

It's no the loss o' warl's gear   *worldly goods*
That could sae bitter draw the tear,
Or mak our Bardie, dowie, wear   *sad*
        The mourning weed:
He's lost a friend and neebor dear,
        In Mailie dead.

Thro' a' the toun she trotted by him;   *farm*
A lang half-mile she could descry him;
Wi' kindly bleat, when she did spy him,
        She ran wi' speed:
A friend mair faithfu' ne'er cam nigh him,
        Than Mailie dead.

I wat she was a sheep o' sense,   *wot*
An' could behave hersel wi' mense: *manners*
I'll say't, she never brak a fence
        Thro' thievish greed.
Our Bardie, lanely, keeps the Spence   *parlour*
        Sin' Mailie's dead.

Or, if he wanders up the howe,   *glen*
Her living image in her yowe   *ewe*

knoll   Comes bleating to him, owre the knowe,
         For bits o' bread;
roll   An' down the briny pearls rowe
         For Mailie dead.

offspring; tups   She was nae get o' moorland tips,
matted fleece   Wi' tawted ket, an' hairy hips;
ancestors   For her forbears were brought in ships
         Frae yont the Tweed:
fleece; shears   A bonier fleesh ne'er cross'd the clips
         Than Mailie's dead.

Woe   Wae worth the man wha first did shape
unlucky   That vile, wanchancie thing – a rape!
twist their faces   It maks guid fellows girn an' gape
         Wi' chokin dread;
     An' Robin's bonnet wave wi' crape
         For Mailie dead.

     O, a' ye Bards on bonie Doon!
     An' wha on Ayr your chanters tune!
     Come, join the melancholious croon
         O' Robin's reed!
above it   His heart will never get aboon!
         His Mailie's dead!

TO JAMES SMITH

Friendship! mysterious cement of the soul!
Sweetner of Life. and solder of Society!
I owe thee much. –

BLAIR

Dear Smith, the sleest, paukie thief,   slyest,
That e'er attempted stealth or rief,   humorous
Ye surely hae some warlock-breef   plunder
         Owre human hearts;   wizard-spell
For ne'er a bosom yet was prief   proof
         Against your arts.

For me, I swear by sun an' moon,
And ev'ry star that blinks aboon,   above
Ye've cost me twenty pair o' shoon
         Just gaun to see you;   going
And ev'ry ither pair that's done,
         Mair taen I'm wi' you.   taken

That auld, capricious carlin, Nature,   crone
To mak amends for scrimpet stature, stunted
She's turn'd you off, a human creature
         On her first plan,
And in her freaks, on ev'ry feature,
         She's wrote, *the Man*.

Just now I've taen the fit o' rhyme,
My barmie noddle's working prime,   fermenting
My fancy yerkit up sublime   brain
         Wi' hasty summon: jerked
Hae ye a leisure-moment's time
         To hear what's comin?

Some rhyme a neebor's name to lash;
Some rhyme (vain thought!) for needfu' cash;
country gossip   Some rhyme to court the countra clash,
     An' raise a din;
trouble about   For me, an aim I never fash;
     I rhyme for fun.

The star that rules my luckless lot,
Has fated me the russet coat,
An' damn'd my fortune to the groat;
     But, in requit,
Has blest me wi' a random shot
     O' countra wit.

turn   This while my notion's taen a sklent,
print   To try my fate in guid, black prent;
Softly!   But still the mair I'm that way bent,
warn; heed   Something cries, 'Hoolie!
'I red you, honest man, tak tent!
     'Ye'll shaw your folly.

'There's ither poets, much your betters,
'Far seen in Greek, deep men o' letters,
'Hae thought they had ensur'd their debtors,
     'A' future ages;
'Now moths deform, in shapeless tatters,
     'Their unknown pages.'

Then farewel hopes o' laurel-boughs,
To garland my poetic brows!
Henceforth I'll rove where busy ploughs
busily   Are whistling thrang,

An' teach the lanely heights an' howes   hollows
               My rustic sang.

I'll wander on, with tentless heed   careless
How never-halting moments speed,
Till fate shall snap the brittle thread;
               Then, all unknown,
I'll lay me with th' inglorious dead,
               Forgot and gone!

But why o' Death begin a tale?
Just now we're living, sound an' hale;
Then top and maintop croud the sail,
               Heave Care o'er-side!
And large, before Enjoyment's gale,
               Let's tak the tide.

This life, sae far's I understand,
Is a' enchanted fairy-land,
Where Pleasure is the Magic Wand,
               That, wielded right,
Maks Hours like Minutes, hand in hand,
               Dance by fu' light.

The magic-wand then let us wield;
For, ance that five-an'-forty's speel'd,   climbed
See, crazy, weary, joyless Eild,   Age
               Wi' wrinkl'd face,
Comes hostin, hirplin owre the field,   coughing,
               Wi' creepin pace.   limping

When ance life's day draws near the gloamin,
Then fareweel vacant, careless roamin;

An' fareweel chearfu' tankards foamin,
                    An' social noise:
An' fareweel dear, deluding woman,
                    The joy of joys!

O Life! how pleasant in thy morning,
Young Fancy's rays the hills adorning!
Cold–pausing Caution's lesson scorning,
                    We frisk away,
Like school-boys, at th' expected warning,
                    To joy and play.

We wander there, we wander here,
We eye the rose upon the brier,
Unmindful that the thorn is near,
                    Among the leaves;
And tho' the puny wound appear,
                    Short while it grieves.

Some, lucky, find a flow'ry spot,
sweated For which they never toil'd nor swat;
They drink the sweet and eat the fat,
Without   But care or pain;
And, haply, eye the barren hut
                    With high disdain.

With steady aim, some Fortune chase;
Keen hope does ev'ry sinew brace;
Thro' fair, thro' foul, they urge the race,
                    And seize the prey:
quietly;
snug Then canie, in some cozie place,
                    They close the day.

To James Smith

And others, like your humble servan',
Poor wights! nae rules nor roads observin;
To right or left, eternal swervin,
          They zig-zag on;
Till, curst with age, obscure an' starvin,
          They aften groan.

Alas! what bitter toil an' straining –
But truce with peevish, poor complaining!
Is Fortune's fickle *Luna* waning?
          E'en let her gang!   go
Beneath what light she has remaining,
          Let's sing our sang.

My pen I here fling to the door,
And kneel, 'Ye Pow'rs!' and warm implore,
'Tho' I should wander *Terra* o'er,
          'In all her climes,
'Grant me but this, I ask no more,
          'Ay rowth o' rhymes.   plenty

'Gie dreeping roasts to countra Lairds,   dripping
'Till icicles hing frae their beards;
'Gie fine braw claes to fine Life-guards   clothes
          'And Maids of Honor;
'And yill an' whisky gie to Cairds,   ale; tinkers
          'Until they sconner.   loathe it

'A Title, Dempster merits it;
'A Garter gie to Willie Pitt;
'Gie Wealth to some be-ledger'd Cit,
          'In cent. per cent.;
'But give me real, sterling Wit,
          'And I'm content.

To James Smith

'While Ye are pleas'd to keep me hale,
'I'll sit down o'er my scanty meal,
'Be't water-brose, or muslin-kail,
    'Wi' chearfu' face,
'As lang's the Muses dinna fail
      'To say the grace.'

brose made
with water;
thin broth

An anxious e'e I never throws
Behint my lug. or by my nose;
I jouk beneath Misfortune's blows
    As weel's I may;
Sworn foe to Sorrow, Care, and Prose,
    I rhyme away.

ear
duck

O ye douce folk, that live by rule,
Grave, tideless-blooded, calm and cool,
Compar'd wi' you – O fool! fool! fool!
    How much unlike!
Your hearts are just a standing pool,
    Your lives, a dyke!

sober

wall

Nae hair-brain'd, sentimental traces,
In your unletter'd, nameless faces!
In *arioso* trills and graces
    Ye never stray,
But *gravissímo*, solemn basses
    Ye hum away.

Ye are sae grave, nae doubt ye're wise;
Nae ferly tho' ye do despise
The hairum-scairum, ram-stam boys,
    The rattling squad:
I see you upward cast your eyes –
    – Ye ken the road. –

wonder
headlong

60

To James Smith

Whilst I – but I shall haud me there –   hold
Wi' you I'll scarce gang ony where –
Then, Jamie, I shall say nae mair,
                 But quat my sang.   quit
Content with You to mak a pair,
                 Whare'er I gang.

THE VISION

The sun had clos'd the winter day,
quitted   The Curlers quat their roaring play,
hare   And hunger'd Maukin taen her way
kitchen-
gardens   To kail-yards green,
each   While faithless snaws ilk step betray
           Whare she has been.

flail   The Thresher's weary flingin-tree,
live-long   The lee-lang day had tired me;
And whan the Day had clos'd his e'e,
           Far i' the West,
Back;
parlour   Ben i' the Spence, right pensivelie,
           I gaed to rest.

-side   There, lanely, by the ingle-cheek,
vomiting
smoke   I sat and ey'd the spewing reek,
cough-;
smoke   That fill'd, wi' hoast-provoking smeek,
building   The auld, clay biggin;
rats   And heard the restless rattons squeak
roof   About the riggin.

dusty   All in this mottie, misty clime,
I backward mus'd on wasted time,
How I had spent my youthfu' prime,
           An' done nae-thing,
nonsense   But stringin blethers up in rhyme,
           For fools to sing.

1. *Duan*, a term of Ossian's for the different divisions of a digressive Poem. See his *Cath-Loda*, vol. 2 of McPherson's Translation.

The Vision

Had I to guid advice but harkit,   harkened
I might, by this, hae led a market,
Or strutted in a Bank and clarkit
        My cash-account:
While here, half-mad, half-fed, half-sarkit,   -shirted
        Is a' th' amount.

I started, mutt'ring blockhead! coof!   fool
And heav'd on high my waukit loof,   hardened palm
To swear by a' yon starry roof,
        Or some rash aith,   oath
That I, henceforth, would be rhyme-proof
        Till my last breath –

When click! the string the snick did draw;   latch
And jee! the door gaed to the wa';
And by my ingle-lowe I saw,   -flame
        Now bleezin bright,
A tight, outlandish Hizzie, braw,   young woman
        Come full in sight.

Ye need na doubt, I held my whisht;   peace
The infant aith, half-form'd, was crusht;
I glowr'd as eerie's I'd been dusht   stared; pushed against
        In some wild glen;
When sweet, like modest Worth, she blusht,
        And stepped ben.   inside

Green, slender, leaf-clad Holly-boughs
Were twisted, gracefu', round her brows,
I took her for some Scottish Muse,
        By that same token;
And come to stop those reckless vows,
        Would soon been broken.

*   *   *   *

The following POEM will, by many readers, be well enough under-
stood; but, for the sake of those who are unacquainted with the
manners and traditions of the country where the scene is cast, Notes
are added, to give some account of the principal Charms and Spells
of that Night, so big with Prophecy to the Peasantry in the West of
Scotland. The passion of prying into Futurity makes a striking part
of the history of Human Nature, in its rude state, in all ages and
nations; and it may be some entertainment to a philosophic mind, if
any such should honour the Author with a perusal, to see the remains
of it, among the more unenlightened in our own.

HALLOWEEN[1]

Yes! let the Rich deride, the Proud disdain,
The simple pleasures of the lowly train;
To me more dear, congenial to my heart,
One native charm, than all the gloss of art.

GOLDSMITH

I

Upon that night, when Fairies light,
    On Cassilis Downans[2] dance,
leas   Or owre the lays, in spendid blaze,
    On sprightly coursers prance;
Or for Colean the rout is taen,
    Beneath the moon's pale beams;
There, up the Cove,[3] to stray an' rove,
    Amang the rocks an' streams
            To sport that night.

1. Is thought to be a night when Witches, Devils, and other
mischief-making beings, are all abroad on their baneful midnight
errands; particularly, those aerial people, the Fairies, are said, on that
night, to hold a grand Anniversary.

2. Certain little, romantic, rocky, green hills, in the neighbour-
hood of the ancient seat of the Earls of Cassilis.

3. A noted cavern near Colean-house, called the Cove of Colean;
which, as well as Cassilis Downans, is famed, in country story, for
being a favourite haunt of Fairies.

II

Amang the bonie, winding banks,
    Where Doon rins, wimplin, clear,   *rippling*
Where BRUCE[1] ance rul'd the martial ranks,
    An' shook his Carrick spear,
Some merry, friendly, countra folks
    Together did convene,
To burn their nits, an' pou their stocks,   *nuts; pull*
    An' haud their Halloween   *hold*
              Fu' blythe that night.

III

The lassies feat, an' cleanly neat,   *trim*
    Mair braw than when they're fine;   *handsome*
Their faces blythe fu' sweetly kythe   *make known*
    Hearts leal, an' warm, an' kin':   *loyal*
The lads sae trig, wi' wooer-babs,   *love-knots*
    Weel knotted on their garten,   *garters*
Some unco blate, an' some wi' gabs,   *shy; chatter*
    Gar lasses hearts gang startin   *Make*
             Whyles fast at night.   *Sometimes*

IV

Then, first an' foremost, thro' the kail,   *greens*
    Their stocks[2] maun a' be sought ance;
They steek their een, an' grape an' wale,   *shut; eyes; grope; choose*

1. The famous family of that name, the ancestors of Robert the great Deliverer of his country, were Earls of Carrick.

2. The first ceremony of Halloween is, pulling each a *Stock*, or plant of kail. They must go out, hand in hand, with eyes shut, and pull the first they meet with: its being big or little, straight or crooked, is prophetic of the size and shape of the grand object of all their Spells – the husband or wife. If any *yird*, or earth, stick to the root, that is *tocher*, or fortune; and the taste of the *custoc*, that is, the heart of the stem, is indicative of the natural temper and disposition.

big; straight	For muckle anes, an' straught anes.
daft; lost the way	Poor hav'rel Will fell aff the drift,
cabbage	An' wandered thro' the Bow-kail,
pulled	An' pow't, for want o' better shift,
stalk	A runt was like a sow-tail,
bent	Sae bow't that night.

V

earth	Then, straught or crooked, yird or nane,
confusedly	They roar an' cry a' throu'ther;
	The vera wee-things, toddlin, rin,
over; shoulder	Wi' stocks out-owre their shouther:
if; pith	An' gif the custock's sweet or sour,
pocket-knives	Wi' joctelegs they taste them;
Then; above	Syne coziely, aboon the door,
cautious	Wi' cannie care, they've plac'd them
	To lie that night.

VI

stole	The lasses staw frae 'mang them a',
	To pou their stalks o' corn[1];
dodges	But Rab slips out, an' jinks about,
big	Behint the muckle thorn:
	He grippet Nelly hard an' fast;

Lastly, the stems, or, to give them their ordinary appellation, the *runts*, are placed somewhere above the head of the door; and the Christian names of the people whom chance brings into the house, are, according to the priority of placing the *runts*, the names in question.

1. They go to the barn-yard, and pull each, at three several times, a stalk of Oats. If the third stalk wants the *top pickle*, that is the grain at the top of the stalk, the party in question will come to the marriage-bed any thing but a Maid.

Loud skirl'd a' the lasses;   *screamed*
But her tap-pickle maist was lost,   *almost*
  When kiutlin in the Fause-house[1]   *cuddling*
          Wi' him that night.

VII

The auld Guidwife's weel-hoordet nits[2] *mistress of the house; well-hoarded*
  Are round an' round divided,
An' monie lads an' lasses fates
  Are there that night decided:
Some kindle, couthie, side by side,   *snugly*
  An' burn thegither trimly;
Some start awa, wi' saucy pride,
  An' jump out-owre the chimlie   *chimney*
          Fu' high that night.

VIII

Jean slips in twa, wi' tentie e'e;   *watchful*
  Wha 'twas, she wadna tell;
But this is *Jock*, an' this is *me*,
  She says in to hersel:
He bleez'd owre her, an' she owre him,
  As they wad never mair part,
Till fuff! he started up the lum,   *chimney*
  An' Jean had e'en a sair heart
          To see't that night.

1. When the corn is in a doubtful state, by being too green, or wet, the stack-builder, by means of old timber, &c. makes a large apartment in his stack, with an opening in the side which is fairest exposed to the wind: this he calls a *Fause house*.

2. Burning the nuts is a favourite charm. They name the lad and lass to each particular nut, as they lay them in the fire; and according as they burn quietly together, or start from beside one another, the course and issue of the Courtship will be.

IX

Poor Willie, wi' his bow-kail runt,
    Was burnt wi' prImsie Mallie;   *prim*
An' Mary, nae doubt, took the drunt,   *huff*
    To be compar'd to Willie:
Mall's nit lap out, wi' pridefu' fling,   *leapt*
    An' her ain fit it brunt it;   *foot*
While Willie lap, an' swoor by jing,   *swore*
    'Twas just the way he wanted
            To be that night.

X

Nell had the Fause-house in her min',
    She pits hersel an' Rob in;   *puts*
In loving bleeze they sweetly join,
    Till white in ase they're sobbin: *ashes*
Nell's heart was dancin at the view;
    She whisper'd Rob to leuk for't:
Rob, stownlins, prie'd her bonie mou,   *by stealth, kissed*
    Fu' cozie in the neuk for't,   *corner*
            Unseen that night.

XI

But Merran sat behint their backs,
    Her thoughts on Andrew Bell;
She lea'es them gashin at their cracks,   *leaves; gossiping; talks*
    An' slips out by hersel:
She thro' the yard the nearest taks,
    An' to the kiln she goes then,
An' darklins grapit for the bauks,   *groped beams*
    And in the blue-clue[1] throws then,
            Right fear't that night.

1. Whoever would, with success, try this spell, must strictly observe these directions: Steal out, all alone, to the *kiln*, and,

XII

An' ay she win't, an' ay she swat,
   I wat she made nae jaukin;
Till something held within the pat,
   Guid Lord! but she was quaukin!
But whether 'twas the Deil himsel,
   Or whether 'twas a bauk-en',
Or whether it was Andrew Bell,
   She did na wait on talkin
                To spier that night.

wound;
sweated
know;
trifling
pot

beam-end

ask

XIII

Wee Jenny to her Graunie says,
   'Will ye go wi' me, Graunie?
'I'll eat the apple[1] at the glass,
   'I gat frae uncle Johnie:'
She fuff't her pipe wi' sic a lunt,
   In wrath she was sae vap'rin,
She notic't na, an aizle brunt
   Her braw new worset apron
                Out thro' that night.

puffed;
smoke

cinder
burned
worsted

XIV

'Ye little Skelpie-limmer's face!
   'I daur ye try sic sportin,

mischievous
hussy's
dare

darkling, throw into the *pot* a clew of blue yarn; wind it in a new clew off the old one; and, towards the latter end, something will hold the thread: demand, *wha hauds?* i.e. who holds; and answer will be returned from the kiln-pot, by naming the Christian and Sirname of your future Spouse.

1. Take a candle, and go alone to a looking-glass; eat an apple before it, and some traditions say, you should comb your hair all the time; the face of your conjugal companion, *to be*, will be seen in the glass, as if peeping over your shoulder.

Halloween

'As seek the foul Thief onie place,
 'For him to spae your fortune:
'Nae doubt but ye may get a sight!
 'Great cause ye hae to fear it;
'For monie a ane has gotten a fright,
 'An' liv'd an' di'd deleeret,
   'On sic a night.

Devil (As seek the foul Thief)
tell (spae)
delirious (deleeret)

XV

'Ae Hairst afore the Sherra-moor,
 'I mind't as weel's yestreen,
'I was a gilpey then, I'm sure
 'I was na past fyfteen:
'The Simmer had been cauld an' wat,
 'An' stuff was unco green;
'An' ay a rantin kirn we gat,
 'An' just on Halloween
   'It fell that night.

harvest;
Sheriffmuir
remember;
last night
girl
wet
grain;
uncommonly
rollicking
harvest-
home

XVI

'Our Stibble-rig was Rab M'Graen,
 'A clever, sturdy fallow;
'His Sin gat Eppie Sim wi' wean,
 'That liv'd in Achmacalla:
'He gat hemp-seed,[1] I mind it weel,

leading
reaper
son; child

---

1. Steal out unperceived, and sow a handful of hemp-seed; harrowing it with anything you can conveniently draw after you. Repeat, now and then, 'Hemp-seed I saw thee, Hemp-seed I saw thee; and him (or her) that is to be my true-love, come after me and pou thee.' Look over your left shoulder, and you will see the appearance of the person invoked, in the attitude of pulling hemp. Some traditions say, 'come after me and shaw thee,' that is, show thyself; in which case it simply appears. Others omit the harrowing, and say, 'come after me and harrow thee.'

'An' he made unco light o't;
'But monie a day was by himsel,   beside
  'He was sae sairly frighted
          'That vera night.'

XVII

Then up gat fechtin Jamie Fleck,   fighting
  An' he swoor by his conscience,
That he could saw hemp-seed a peck;   sow
  For it was a' but nonsense:
The auld guidman raught down the pock,   reached; bag
  An' out a handfu' gied him;
Syne bad him slip frae 'mang the folk,   Then
  Sometime when nae ane see'd him,
          An' try't that night.

XVIII

He marches thro' amang the stacks,
  Tho' he was something sturtin;   frightened
The graip he for a harrow taks,   dung fork
  An' haurls at his curpin: drags; crupper
And ev'ry now an' then, he says,
  'Hemp-seed I saw thee,   sow
'An' her that is to be my lass
  'Come after me an' draw thee
          'As fast this night.'

XIX

He whistl'd up Lord Lenox' march,
  To keep his courage cheary;
Altho' his hair began to arch,
  He was sae fley'd an' eerie: scared
Till presently he hears a squeak,

groan An' then a grane an' gruntle;
shoulder; He by his shouther gae a keek,
    look
stagger An' tumbl'd wi' a wintle
                    Out-owre that night.

XX

He roar'd a horrid murder-shout,
    In dreadfu' desperation!
An' young an' auld come rinnin out,
    An' hear the sad narration:
limping He swoor 'twas hilchin Jean M'Craw,
crook-   Or crouchie Merran Humphie,
backed
    Till stop! she trotted thro' them a';
the pig An' wha was it but *Grumphie*
Astir   Asteer that night!

XXI

have gone Meg fain wad to the Barn gaen,
winnow   To winn three wechts o' naething;[1]
alone But for to meet the Deil her lane,
    She pat but little faith in:
put She gies the Herd a pickle nits,
shepherd;   An' twa red cheekit apples,
few
To watch, while for the barn she sets,
    In hopes to see Tam Kipples
                    That vera night.

1. This charm must likewise be performed, unperceived and alone. You go to the *barn*, and open both doors, taking them off the hinges, if possible; for there is danger, that the *being*, about to appear may shut the doors, and do you some mischief. Then take that instrument used in winnowing the corn, which, in our country-dialect, we call a *wecht*; and go through all the attitudes of letting down corn against the wind. Repeat it three times; and the third time, an apparition will pass through the barn, in at the windy door, and out at the other, having both the figure in question, and the appearance or retinue, marking the employment or station in life.

XXII

She turns the key, wi' cannie thraw,   cautious
   An' owre the threshold ventures;   twist
But first on Sawnie gies a ca',   call
   Syne bauldly in she enters: Then boldly
A ratton rattl'd up the wa',   rat
   An' she cry'd, Lord preserve her!
An' ran thro' midden-hole an' a',   dung-hill
   An' pray'd wi' zeal and fervour,
               Fu' fast that night.

XXIII

They hoy't out Will, wi' sair advice;   urged
   They hecht him some fine braw ane;   promised
It chanc'd the Stack he faddom't thrice,[1]
   Was timmer-propt for thrawin;   timber-; against bending
He taks a swirlie, auld moss-oak,   gnarled
   For some black, grousome Carlin;   old woman
An' loot a winze, an' drew a stroke,   let out an oath
   Till skin in blypes cam haurlin   shreds; peeling
               Aff's nieves that night.   Off his fists

XXIV

A wanton widow Leezie was,
   As cantie as a kittlen;   lively; kitten
But, Och! that night, amang the shaws,   woods
   She gat a fearfu' settlin!
She thro' the whins, an' by the cairn,

---

1. Take an opportunity of going, unnoticed, to a *Bearstack*, and fathom it three times round. The last fathom of the last time, you will catch in your arms the appearance of your future conjugal yoke-fellow.

An' owre the hill gaed scrievin,
 Whare three Lairds' lands met at a burn,[1]
  To dip her left sark-sleeve in,
    Was bent that night.

careering

shift-

XXV

Whyles owre a linn the burnie plays,
 As thro' the glen it wimpl't;
Whyles round a rocky scar it strays;
 Whyles in a wiel it dimpl't;
Whyles glitter'd to the nightly rays,
 Wi' bickering, dancing dazzle;
Whyles cookit underneath the braes,
 Below the spreading hazle
    Unseen that night.

Now; fall

rippled

eddy

hid

XXVI

Amang the brachens, on the brae,
 Between her an' the moon,
The Deil, or else an outler Quey,
 Gat up an' gae a croon:
Poor Leezie's heart maist lap the hool;
 Near lav'rock-height she jumpit,
But mist a fit, an' in the pool
 Out-owre the lugs she plumpit,
    Wi' a plunge that night.

young cow in the field

almost leaped out of her skin lark-high

foot

ears

1. You go out, one or more, for this is a social spell, to a south-running spring or rivulet, where 'three Lairds' lands meet,' and dip your left shirt-sleeve. Go to bed in sight of a fire, and hang your wet sleeve before it to dry. Lie awake; and, some time near midnight, an apparition, having the exact figure of the grand object in question, will come and turn the sleeve, as if to dry the other side of it.

XXVII

In order, on the clean hearth-stane,
   The Luggies three[1] are ranged;   *wooden dishes*
And ev'ry time great care is taen,
   To see them duly changed:
Auld uncle John, wha wedlock's joys
   Sin Mar's-year did desire,   *1715, Mar's rising*
Because he gat the toom dish thrice,   *empty*
   He heav'd them on the fire
             In wrath that night.

XXVIII

Wi' merry sangs, an' friendly cracks,
   I wat they did na weary;   *wot*
And unco tales, an' funnie jokes,   *wondrous*
   Their sports were cheap an' cheary:
Till butter'd So'ns,[2] wi' fragrant lunt,   *porridge made from siftings of oats; steam*
   Set a' their gabs a-steerin;   *tongues wagging*
Syne, wi' a social glass o' strunt,   *liquor*
   They parted aff careerin
             Fu' blythe that night.

---

1. Take three dishes; put clean water in one, foul water in another, leave the third empty: blind-fold a person, and lead him to the hearth where the dishes are ranged; he (or she) dips the left hand: if by chance in the clean water, the future husband or wife will come to the bar of Matrimony a maid; if in the foul, a widow; if in the empty dish, it foretells, with equal certainty, no marriage at all. It is repeated three times; and every time the arrangement of the dishes is altered.

2. Sowens, with butter instead of milk to them, is always the *Hallowein Supper*.

THE AULD FARMER'S NEW-YEAR MORNING SALUTATION TO HIS AULD MARE, MAGGIE,

ON GIVING HER THE ACCUSTOMED RIPP OF CORN TO HANSEL IN THE NEW-YEAR

A *Guid New-year* I wish thee, Maggie!
Hae, there's a ripp to thy auld baggie:
Tho' thou's howe-backit, now, an' knaggie,
    I've seen the day,
Thou could hae gaen like onie staggie
      Out-owre the lay.

Tho' now thou's dowie, stiff, an' crazy,
An' thy auld hide as white's a daisie,
I've seen thee dappl't, sleek an' glaizie,
    A bonie gray:
He should been tight that daur't to raize thee,
      Ance in a day.

Thou ance was i' the foremost rank,
A filly buirdly, steeve, an' swank,
An' set weel down a shapely shank,
    As e'er tread yird;
An' could hae flown out-owre a stank,
      Like onie bird.

It's now some nine-an'-twenty year,
Sin' thou was my Guid-father's Meere;
He gied me thee, o' tocher clear,
    An' fifty mark;
Tho' it was sma', 'twas weel-won gear,
      An' thou was stark.

76

New-Year Morning Salutation

When first I gaed to woo my Jenny,
Ye then was trottin wi' your Minnie: *mother*
Tho' ye was trickie, slee, an' funnie,   *sly*
        Ye ne'er was donsie;   *vicious*
But hamely, tawie, quiet, an' cannie,   *tractable;*
        An' unco sonsie.   *easy*
                        good-natured

That day, ye pranc'd wi' muckle pride,
When ye bure hame my bonie Bride;   *bore*
An' sweet an' gracefu' she did ride,
        Wi' maiden air!
Kyle Stewart[1] I could bragged wide,   *have challenged*
        For sic a pair.

Tho' now ye dow but hoyte and hoble,   *can; amble crazily; stumble*
An' wintle like a saumont-coble,   *rock; salmon-boat*
That day, ye was a jinker noble,   *racer*
        For heels an' win'!   *wind*
An' ran them till they a' did wauble,   *wobble*
        Far, far behin'!

When thou an' I were young an' skiegh,   *skittish*
An' stable-meals at Fairs were driegh,   *dreary*
How thou wad prance, an' snore, an' skriegh,   *snort; whinny*
        An' tak the road!
Town's-bodies ran, an' stood abiegh,   *-folk; out of the way*
        An' ca't thee mad.

When thou was corn't, an' I was mellow,
We took the road ay like a Swallow:
At Brooses thou had ne'er a fellow,   *Wedding-races*
        For pith an' speed;

---

1. Northern part of Kyle, Burns's district in Ayrshire. – EDD.

beat

But ev'ry tail thou pay't them hollow,
　　　　Whare'er thou gaed.

-rumped
perhaps have
beaten;
spurt
made;
wheeze
switch
willow

The sma', droop-rumpl't, hunter cattle,
Might aiblins waur't thee for a brattle;
But sax Scotch miles thou try't their mettle,
　　　　An' gar't them whaizle:
Nae whip nor spur, but just a wattle
　　　　O' saugh or hazle.

leather or
rope trace
eight; going

six; by
ourselves

Thou was a noble Fittie-lan',[1]
As e'er in tug or tow was drawn!
Aft thee an' I, in aught hours gaun,
　　　　On guid March-weather,
Hae turn'd sax rood beside our han',
　　　　For days thegither.

plunged;
jerked;
fretted

breast

tough-rooted
hillocks
would have
roared;
cracked
fallen gently
over

Thou never braindg't, an' fetch't, an' fliskit,
But thy auld tail thou wad hae whiskit,
An' spread abreed thy weel-fill'd brisket,
　　　　Wi' pith an' pow'r,
Till spritty knowes wad rair't an' riskit,
　　　　An' slypet owre.

wooden dish

wood

knew
Without that,
till Summer

When frosts lay lang, an' snaws were deep,
An' threaten'd labor back to keep,
I gied thy cog a wee-bit heap
　　　　Aboon the timmer;
I ken'd my Maggie wad na sleep
　　　　For that, or Simmer.

1. Rear left-hand horse in a plough, which treads on the un-
ploughed land. – EDD.

New-Year Morning Salutation

In cart or car thou never reestit; *refused to go*
The steyest brae thou wad hae fac't it; *stiffest*
Thou never lap, an' sten't an' breastit, *leaped; reared; sprang forward*
        Then stood to blaw;
But just thy step a wee thing hastit,
        Thou snoov't awa. *jogged along*

My Pleugh is now thy bairn-time a'; *team; offspring*
Four gallant brutes as e'er did draw;
Forbye sax mae, I've sell't awa, *Besides; more*
        That thou hast nurst:
They drew me thretteen pund an' twa,
        The vera warst.

Monie a sair daurk we twa hae wrought, *day's work*
An' wi' the weary warl' fought! *world*
An' monie an anxious day, I thought
        We wad be beat!
Yet here to crazy Age we're brought,
        Wi' something yet.

An' think na, my auld, trusty Servan',
That now perhaps thou's less deservin,
An' thy auld days may end in starvin',
        For my last fou, *bushel*
A heapet Stimpart, I'll reserve ane *quarter-peck*
        Laid by for you. *aside*

We've worn to crazy years thegither; *lived*
We'll toyte about wi' ane anither; *totter*
Wi' tentie care I'll flit thy tether, *attentive; change*
        To some hain'd rig, *reserved field*
Whare ye may nobly rax your leather, *stretch*
        Wi' sma' fatigue.

THE COTTER'S SATURDAY NIGHT

INSCRIBED TO R. AIKEN, ESQ.

Let not Ambition mock their useful toil,
Their homely joys and destiny obscure;
Nor Grandeur hear, with a disdainful smile,
The short but simple annals of the Poor.

GRAY

I

My lov'd, my honor'd, much respected friend!
 No mercenary Bard his homage pays;
With honest pride, I scorn each selfish end,
 My dearest meed, a friend's esteem and praise:
To you I sing, in simple Scottish lays,
The lowly train in life's sequester'd scene;
 The native feelings strong, the guileless ways,
What Aiken in a Cottage would have been;
Ah! tho' his worth unknown, far happier there, I
  ween!

II

moan   November chill blaws loud wi' angry sugh;
 The short'ning winter-day is near a close;
The miry beasts retreating frae the pleugh;
 The black'ning trains o' craws to their repose:
The toil-worn Cotter frae his labor goes,
This night his weekly moil is at an end,
 Collects his spades, his mattocks, and his hoes,
Hoping the morn in ease and rest to spend,
And weary, o'er the moor, his course does hame-
  ward bend.

80

III

At length his lonely Cot appears in view,
    Beneath the shelter of an aged tree;
Th' expectant wee-things, toddlin, stacher through   totter
    To meet their Dad, wi' flichterin noise and glee.   fluttering
    His wee-bit ingle, blinkin bonilie,
His clean hearth-stane, his thrifty Wifie's smile,
    The lisping infant, prattling on his knee,
Does a' his weary carking cares beguile,
And makes him quite forget his labor and his toil.

IV

Belyve, the elder bairns come drapping in,   By-and-by
    At service out, amang the Farmers roun';
Some ca' the pleugh, some herd, some tentie rin   drive; heedful run
    A cannie errand to a neebor town: easy
    Their eldest hope, their Jenny, woman grown,
In youthfu' bloom, Love sparkling in her e'e,
    Comes hame, perhaps, to shew a braw new gown,
Or deposite her sair-won penny-fee,   hard-; wages
To help her Parents dear, if they in hardship be.

V

With joy unfeign'd, brothers and sisters meet,
    And each for other's weelfare kindly spiers: asks
The social hours, swift-wing'd, unnotic'd fleet;
    Each tells the uncos that he sees or hears.   uncommon things
    The Parents, partial, eye their hopeful years;
Anticipation forward points the view;
    The Mother, wi' her needle and her sheers,
Gars auld claes look amaist as weel's the new;   Makes; clothes; almost
The Father mixes a' wi' admonition due.

VI

Their Master's and their Mistress's command,
    The youngkers a' are warned to obey;
diligent And mind their labors wi' an eydent hand,
   idle And ne'er, tho' out o' sight, to jauk or play:
    'And O! be sure to fear the Lord alway!
    'And mind your duty, duely, morn and night!
    'Lest in temptation's path ye gang astray,
    'Implore his counsel and assisting might:
    'They never sought in vain that sought the Lord
       aright.'

VII

But hark! a rap comes gently to the door;
    Jenny, wha kens the meaning o' the same,
Tells how a neebor lad cam o'er the moor,
    To do some errands, and convoy her hame.
    The wily Mother sees the conscious flame
Sparkle in Jenny's e'e, and flush her cheek,
    With heart-struck, anxious care, enquires his name,
  half While Jenny hafflins is afraid to speak;
    Weel pleas'd the Mother hears, it's nae wild, worthless Rake.

VIII

    in With kindly welcome, Jenny brings him ben;
    A strappan youth, he takes the Mother's eye;
Blythe Jenny sees the visit's no ill taen;
chats; cattle The Father cracks of horses, pleughs, and kye.
    The Youngster's artless heart o'erflows wi' joy,
shy;
sheepish But blate and laithfu', scarce can weel behave;
    The Mother, wi' a woman's wiles, can spy

What makes the Youth sae bashfu' and sae grave;
Weel-pleas'd to think her bairn's respected like the
    lave.   rest

IX

O happy love! where love like this is found!
    O heart-felt raptures! bliss beyond compare!
I've paced much this weary, mortal round,
    And sage Experience bids me this declare –
    'If Heaven a draught of heavenly pleasure spare,
'One cordial in this melancholy Vale,
    ' 'Tis when a youthful, loving, modest Pair,
'In other's arms, breathe out the tender tale,
'Beneath the milk-white thorn that scents
        the ev'ning gale.'

X

Is there, in human form, that bears a heart –
    A Wretch! a Villain! lost to love and truth!
That can, with studied, sly, ensnaring art,
    Betray sweet Jenny's unsuspecting youth?
    Curse on his perjur'd arts! dissembling smooth!
Are Honor, Virtue, Conscience, all exil'd?
    Is there no Pity, no relenting Ruth,
Points to the Parents fondling o'er their Child?
Then paints the ruin'd Maid, and their distraction
    wild!

XI

But now the Supper crowns their simple board,   wholesome
    The healsome Parritch, chief of Scotia's food:
The soupe their only Hawkie does afford,   sup: cow
    That 'yont the hallan snugly chows her cood: beyond; partition

-saved cheese, strong

The Dame brings forth, in complimental mood,
 To grace the lad, her weel-hain'd kebbuck, fell,
  And aft he's prest, and aft he ca's it guid;
 The frugal Wifie, garrulous, will tell,

twelve-month; flax; flower

How 'twas a towmond auld, sin' Lint was i' the bell.

XII

The chearfu' Supper done, wi' serious face,
 They, round the ingle, form a circle wide;
The Sire turns o'er ,wi' patriarchal grace,

hall-

  The big ha'-Bible, ance his Father's pride:
 His bonnet rev'rently is laid aside,

grey side-locks

  His lyart haffets wearing thin and bare;
  Those strains that once did sweet in Zion glide,

chooses

He wales a portion with judicious care;
 'And let us worship God!' he says, with solemn air.

XIII

They chant their artless notes in simple guise;
 They tune their hearts, by far the noblest aim:
Perhaps *Dundee's* wild-warbling measures rise,
 Or plaintive *Martyrs*, worthy of the name;

feeds

 Or noble *Elgin* beets the heaven-ward flame,
The sweetest far of Scotia's holy lays:
 Compar'd with these, Italian trills are tame;
The tickl'd ears no heart-felt raptures raise;
Nae unison hae they, with our Creator's praise.

XIV

The priest-like Father reads the sacred page,
 How Abram was the Friend of God on high;
Or, Moses bade eternal warfare wage

With Amalek's ungracious progeny;
   Or how the royal Bard did groaning lye,
Beneath the stroke of Heaven's avenging ire;
   Or Job's pathetic plaint, and wailing cry;
Or rapt Isaiah's wild, seraphic fire;
Or other Holy Seers that tune the sacred lyre.

XV

Perhaps the Christian Volume is the theme,
   How guiltless blood for guilty man was shed;
How He, who bore in heaven the second name,
   Had not on Earth whereon to lay His head:
   How His first followers and servants sped;
The precepts sage they wrote to many a land:
   How he, who lone in Patmos banished,
Saw in the sun a mighty angel stand;
And heard great Bab'lon's doom pronounc'd
     by Heaven's command.

XVI

Then kneeling down to Heaven's Eternal King,
   The Saint, the Father, and the Husband prays:
Hope 'springs exulting on triumphant wing,'[1]
   That thus they all shall meet in future days:
   There, ever bask in uncreated rays,
No more to sigh, or shed the bitter tear,
   Together hymning their Creator's praise,
In such society, yet still more dear;
While circling Time moves round in an eternal
     sphere.

1. Pope's Windsor Forest.

XVII

Compar'd with this, how poor Religion's pride,
   In all the pomp of method, and of art,
When men display to congregations wide,
   Devotion's ev'ry grace, except the heart!
   The Power, incens'd, the Pageant will desert,
The pompous strain, the sacerdotal stole;
   But haply, in some Cottage far apart,
May hear, well-pleas'd, the language of the Soul;
And in His Book of Life the Inmates poor enroll.

XVIII

Then homeward all take off their sev'ral way;
   The youngling Cottagers retire to rest:
The Parent-pair their secret homage pay,
   And proffer up to Heaven the warm request,
   That He who stills the raven's clam'rous nest,
And decks the lily fair in flow'ry pride,
   Would, in the way His Wisdom sees the best,
For them and for their little ones provide;
But chiefly, in their hearts with Grace divine preside.

XIX

From scenes like these, old Scotia's grandeur springs,
   That makes her lov'd at home, rever'd abroad:
Princes and lords are but the breath of kings,
   'An honest man's the noblest work of God:'
   And certes, in fair Virtue's heavenly road,
The Cottage leaves the Palace far behind;
   What is a lordling's pomp! a cumbrous load,
Disguising oft the wretch of human kind,
Studied in arts of Hell, in wickedness refin'd!

XX

O Scotia! my dear, my native soil!
　For whom my warmest wish to Heaven is sent!
Long may thy hardy sons of rustic toil
　Be blest with health, and peace, and sweet content!
　And, O! may Heaven their simple lives prevent
From Luxury's contagion, weak and vile!
　Then, howe'er crowns and coronets be rent,
A virtuous Populace may rise the while,
And stand a wall of fire around their much-lov'd Isle.

XXI

O Thou! who pour'd the patriotic tide,
　That stream'd thro' Wallace's undaunted heart;
Who dar'd to, nobly, stem tyrannic pride,
　Or nobly die, the second glorious part,
　(The Patriot's God, peculiarly thou art,
　His friend, inspirer, guardian, and reward!)
　O never never, Scotia's realm desert,
But still the Patriot, and the Patriot-Bard,
In bright succession raise, her Ornament and Guard!

TO A MOUSE,

ON TURNING HER UP IN HER NEST, WITH
THE PLOUGH, NOVEMBER 1785

Wee, sleekit, cowrin, tim'rous beastie,
O, what a panic's in thy breastie!
hurrying Thou need na start awa sae hasty,
scamper   Wi' bickering brattle!
loath I wad be laith to rin an' chase thee,
plough-staff   Wi' murd'ring pattle!

I'm truly sorry Man's dominion
Has broken Nature's social union,
An' justifies that ill opinion,
      Which makes thee startle,
At me, thy poor, earth-born companion,
      An' fellow-mortal!

sometimes I doubt na, whyles, but thou may thieve;
What then? poor beastie, thou maun live!
odd ear; A daimen icker in a thrave
twenty-four
sheaves   'S a sma' request.
what's left I'll get a blessin wi' the lave,
      An' never miss't!

Thy wee-bit housie, too, in ruin!
feeble Its silly wa's the win's are strewin!
build An' naething, now, to big a new ane,
moss   O' foggage green!
An' bleak December's winds ensuin,
biting   Baith snell an' keen!

To a Mouse

Thou saw the fields laid bare an' waste,
An' weary Winter comin fast,
An' cozie here, beneath the blast,
      Thou thought to dwell,
Till crash! the cruel coulter past
      Out thro' thy cell.

That wee-bit heap o' leaves an' stibble   *stubble*
Has cost thee monie a weary nibble!
Now thou's turn'd out, for a' thy trouble,
      But house or hald,   *Without; holding*
To thole the Winter's sleety dribble,   *endure*
      An' cranreuch cauld!   *hoar-frost*

But, Mousie, thou art no thy lane,   *alone*
In proving foresight may be vain:
The best-laid schemes o' Mice an' Men
      Gang aft a-gley,   *awry*
An' lea'e us nought but grief an' pain,
      For promis'd joy!

Still thou art blest, compar'd wi' me!
The present only toucheth thee:
But, Och! I backward cast my e'e
      On prospects drear!
An' forward, tho' I canna see,
      I guess an' fear!

EPISTLE TO DAVIE,
A BROTHER POET

January —

While winds frae aff Ben-Lomond blaw,
And bar the doors wi' driving snaw,

hang   And hing us owre the ingle,
I set me down, to pass the time,
And spin a verse or twa o' rhyme,

westland   In hamely, westlin jingle.
While frosty winds blaw in the drift,

In to the
chimney
corner   Ben to the chimla lug,
I grudge a wee the Great-folk's gift,

comfortable   That live sae bien an' snug:

heed   I tent less, and want less
             Their roomy fire-side;
           But hanker, and canker,
             To see their cursed pride.

II

It's hardly in a body's pow'r,
To keep, at times, frae being sour,
        To see how things are shar'd;

chaps; some-
times   How best o' chiels are whyles in want,

fools; revel   While Coofs on countless thousands rant,

spend   And ken na how to wair't:

trouble   But Davie, lad, ne'er fash your head,

wealth   Tho' we hae little gear,
We're fit to win our daily bread,

sound   As lang's we're hale and fier:

'Mair spier na, nor fear na',[1]
  Auld age ne'er mind a feg;
The last o't, the warst o't,
  Is only but to beg.

More ask not

fig

III

To lie in kilns and barns at e'en,
When banes are craz'd, and bluid is thin,
  Is, doubtless, great distress!
Yet then content could make us blest;
Ev'n then, sometimes we'd snatch a taste
  Of truest happiness.
The honest heart that's free frae a'
  Intended fraud or guile,
However Fortune kick the ba',
  Has ay some cause to smile,
    And mind still, you'll find still,
      A comfort this nae sma';
    Nae mair then, we'll care then,
      Nae farther we can fa'.

IV

What tho', like Commoners of air,
We wander out, we know not where,
  But either house or hal'?
Yet Nature's charms, the hills and woods,
The sweeping vales, and foaming floods,
  Are free alike to all.
In days when Daisies deck the ground,
  And Blackbirds whistle clear,
With honest joy our hearts will bound,
  To see the coming year:

Without

1. Ramsay.

On braes when we please, then,
   We'll sit an' sowth a tune;
Syne rhyme till't, we'll time till't,
   And sing't when we hae done.

whistle in a
low key
Then

V

It's no in titles nor in rank;
It's no in wealth like Lon'on Bank,
   To purchase peace and rest;
It's no in makin muckle, mair:
It's no in books; it's no in lear,
   To make us truly blest:
If Happiness hae not her seat
   And centre in the breast,
We may be wise, or rich, or great,
   But never can be blest:
     Nae treasures, nor pleasures,
      Could make us happy lang;
     The heart ay's the part ay,
      That makes us right or wrang.

much, more

learning

VI

Think ye, that sic as you and I,
Wha drudge and drive thro' wet and dry,
   Wi' never-ceasing toil;
Think ye, are we less blest than they,
Wha scarcely tent us in their way,
   As hardly worth their while?
Alas! how aft, in haughty mood,
   God's creatures they oppress!
Or else, neglecting a' that's guid,
   They riot in excess!

heed

Baith careless, and fearless,
   Of either Heaven or Hell;
Esteeming and deeming
   It a' an idle tale!

VII

Then let us chearfu' acquiesce;
Nor make our scanty Pleasures less,
  By pining at our state:
And, even should Misfortunes come,
I, here wha sit, hae met wi' some,
  An's thankfu' for them yet.   And am
They gie the wit of Age to Youth;
  They let us ken oursel;
They make us see the naked truth,
  The real guid and ill.
    Tho' losses, and crosses,
      Be lessons right severe,
     There's wit there, ye'll get there,
     Ye'll find nae other where.

VIII

But tent me, Davie, Ace o' Hearts!   attend to
(To say aught less wad wrang the cartes,   cards
  And flatt'ry I detest)
This life has joys for you and I;
And joys that riches ne'er could buy;
  And joys the very best.
There's a' the Pleasures o' the Heart,
  The Lover an' the Frien';
Ye hae your Meg, your dearest part,
  And I my darling Jean!

It warms me, it charms me,
    To mention but her name:
kindles   It heats me, it beets me,
    And sets me a' on flame!

IX

O all ye Pow'rs who rule above!
O Thou, whose very self art love!
    Thou know'st my words sincere!
The life-blood streaming thro' my heart,
Or my more dear Immortal part,
    Is not more fondly dear!
When heart-corroding care and grief
    Deprive my soul of rest,
Her dear idea brings relief,
    And solace to my breast.
    Thou Being, All-seeing,
      O hear my fervent pray'r!
    Still take her, and make her
      Thy most peculiar care!

X

All hail! ye tender feelings dear!
The smile of love, the friendly tear,
    The sympathetic glow;
Long since, this world's thorny ways
Had number'd out my weary days,
    Had it not been for you!
Fate still has blest me with a friend,
    In ev'ry care and ill;
And oft a more endearing band,
    A tie more tender still.

It lightens, it brightens,
    The tenebrific scene,
To meet with, and greet with
    My Davie, or my Jean!

XI

O, how that name inspires my style!
The words come skelpin, rank and file,   rushing
    Amaist before I ken!
The ready measures rins as fine,
As Phœbus and the famous Nine
    Were glowrin owre my pen.   staring
My spaviet Pegasus will limp,   spavined
    Till ance he's fairly het;   hot
And then he'll hilch, and stilt, and jimp,   hobble; limp; jump
    And rin an unco fit: uncommon pace
      But least then, the beast then   lest
        Should rue this hasty ride,
      I'll light now, and dight now   wipe
        His sweaty, wizen'd hide.

TO A MOUNTAIN DAISY,

ON TURNING ONE DOWN, WITH THE PLOUGH, IN APRIL 1786

Wee, modest, crimson-tipped flow'r,
Thou's met me in an evil hour;
For I maun crush amang the stoure
        Thy slender stem:
To spare thee now is past my pow'r,
        Thou bonie gem.

Alas! it's no thy neebor sweet,
The bonnie Lark, companion meet!
Bending thee 'mang the dewy weet!
        Wi' spreckl'd breast,
When upward-springing, blythe, to greet
        The purpling East.

Cauld blew the bitter-biting North
Upon thy early, humble birth;
Yet chearfully thou glinted forth
        Amid the storm,
Scarce rear'd above the Parent-earth
        Thy tender form.

The flaunting flow'rs our Gardens yield,
High shelt'ring woods and wa's maun shield;
But thou, beneath the random bield
        O' clod or stane,
Adorns the histie stibble-field,
        Unseen, alane.

dust (gloss for line 3)

wet (gloss for line 9)

walls must / *shelter* (gloss)

barren stubble- (gloss)

96

To a Mountain Daisy

There, in thy scanty mantle clad,
Thy snawie bosom sun-ward spread,
Thou lifts thy unassuming head
         In humble guise;
But now the share uptears thy bed,
         And low thou lies!

Such is the fate of artless Maid,
Sweet flow'ret of the rural shade!
By Love's simplicity betray'd,
         And guileless trust,
Till she, like thee, all soil'd, is laid
         Low i' the dust.

Such is the fate of simple Bard,
On Life's rough ocean luckless starr'd!
Unskilful he to note the card
         Of prudent Lore,
Till billows rage, and gales blow hard,
         And whelm him o'er!

Such fate to suffering Worth is giv'n,
Who long with wants and woes has striv'n,
By human pride or cunning driv'n
         To Mis'ry's brink,
Till wrench'd of ev'ry stay but Heav'n,
         He, ruin'd, sink!

Ev'n thou who mourn'st the Daisy's fate,
That fate is thine - no distant date;
Stern Ruin's plough-share drives, elate,
         Full on thy bloom,
Till crush'd beneath the furrow's weight,
         Shall be thy doom!

ON A SCOTCH BARD

GONE TO THE WEST INDIES

A' ye wha live by sowps o' drink,

rhyme   A' ye wha live by crambo-clink,

A' ye wha live and never think,
         Come mourn wi' me!

comrade;
the slip   Our billie's gien us a' a jink,
         An' owre the sea.

jovial com-
pany   Lament him a' ye rantin core,

frolic   Wha dearly like a random-splore,

Nae mair he'll join the merry roar,
         In social key;

For now he's taen anither shore,
         An' owre the sea!

wish   The bonie lasses weel may wiss him,

And in their dear petitions place him:

The widows, wives, an' a' may bless him,
         Wi' tearfu' e'e;

wot   For weel I wat they'll sairly miss him
         That's owre the sea!

O Fortune, they hae room to grumble!

blunderer   Hadst thou taen aff some drowsy bummle,

fuss   Wha can do nought but fyke an' fumble,
         'Twad been nae plea;

nimble;
gimlet   But he was gleg as onie wumble,
         That's owre the Sea!

On a Scotch Bard

Auld, cantie Kyle may weepers wear,   cheerful
An' stain them wi' the saut, saut tear: salt
'Twill mak her poor, auld heart, I fear,
        In flinders flee: fragments
He was her Laureat monie a year,
           That's owre the Sea!

He saw Misfortune's cauld Nor-west
Lang mustering up a bitter blast;
A Jillet brak his heart at last,   jilt
        Ill may she be!
So, took a birth afore the mast,
          An' owre the Sea.

To tremble under Fortune's cummock,   cudgel
On scarce a bellyfu' o' drummock,   meal and water
Wi' his proud, independent stomach,
        Could ill agree;
So, row't his hurdies in a hammock,   rolled; buttocks
          An' owre the Sea.

He ne're was gien to great misguiding,
Yet coin his pouches wad na bide in;   pockets
Wi' him it ne'er was under hiding;
        He dealt it free:
The Muse was a' that he took pride in,
          That's owre the Sea.

Jamaica bodies, use him weel,
An' hap him in a cozie biel: wrap; shelter
Ye'll find him ay a dainty chiel,
        An' fou o' glee:
He wad na wrang'd the vera Deil,   would not have
          That's owre the Sea.

On a Scotch Bard

Fareweel, my rhyme-composing billie!
unkind   Your native soil was right ill-willie;
But may ye flourish like a lily,
        Now bonilie!
gill   I'll toast ye in my hindmost gillie,
        Tho' owre the Sea!

TO A LOUSE,

ON SEEING ONE ON A LADY'S BONNET AT CHURCH

Ha! whare ye gaun, ye crowlin ferlie!   *crawling wonder*
Your impudence protects you sairlie:
I canna say but ye strunt rarely,   *strut*
        Owre gauze and lace;
Tho' faith, I fear, ye dine but sparely
        On sic a place.

Ye ugly, creepin, blastit wonner,
Detested, shunn'd, by saunt an' sinner,
How daur ye set your fit upon her,   *foot*
        Sae fine a Lady!
Gae somewhere else and seek your dinner,
        On some poor body.

Swith, in some beggar's haffet squattle;   *Off! temple squat*
There ye may creep, and sprawl, and sprattle   *scramble*
Wi' ither kindred, jumping cattle,
        In shoals and nations;
Whare horn nor bane ne'er daur unsettle
        Your thick plantations.

Now haud you there, ye're out o' sight,   *keep*
Below the fatt'rels, snug and tight;   *falderals*
Na faith ye yet! ye'll no be right
        Till ye've got on it,
The vera tapmost, tow'ring height
        O' Miss's bonnet.

My sooth! right bauld ye set your nose out,
As plump an' gray as onie grozet: *gooseberry*
O for some rank, mercurial rozet,   *rosin*
        Or fell, red smeddum,   *deadly; powder*
I'd gie ye sic a hearty dose o't,
        Wad dress your droddum!   *bottom*

I wad na been surpris'd to spy   *would not have*
You on an auld wife's flainen toy;   *flannel cap*
Or aiblins some bit duddie boy,   *maybe; small ragged*
        On's wyliecoat;   *flannel vest*
But Miss's fine Lunardi! fye!   *balloon bonnet*
        How daur ye do't?

O Jenny, dinna toss your head,
An' set your beauties a' abread!   *abroad*
Ye little ken what cursed speed
        The blastie's makin!
Thae winks and finger-ends, I dread,   *Those*
        Are notice takin!

O wad some Pow'r the giftie gie us
To see oursels as others see us!
It wad frae monie a blunder free us
        An' foolish notion:
What airs in dress an' gait wad lea'e us,
        An' ev'n Devotion!

EPISTLE TO J. LAPRAIK,

AN OLD SCOTTISH BARD

While briers an' woodbines budding green,
And Paitricks scraichin loud at e'en,
An' morning Poussie whiddin seen,
      Inspire my Muse,
This freedom, in an unknown frien',
      I pray excuse.

partridges
screaming
hare
scudding

On Fasten-een we had a rockin,
To ca' the crack and weave our stockin;
And there was muckle fun and jokin,
      Ye need na doubt;
At length we had a hearty yokin
      At sang about.

Shrove
Tuesday;
party
have a chat

set-to

There was ae sang, amang the rest,
Aboon them a' it pleas'd me best,
That some kind husband had addrest
      To some sweet wife:
It thirl'd the heart-strings thro' the breast,
      A' to the life.

thrilled

I've scarce heard ought describ'd sae weel,
What gen'rous, manly bosoms feel;
Thought I, 'Can this be Pope or Steele,
      'Or Beattie's wark?'
They tald me 'twas an odd kind chiel
      About Muirkirk.

fellow

It pat me fidgin-fain to hear't,
An' sae about him there I spier't;
Then a' that ken't him round declar'd,
He had ingine,
That nane excell'd it, few cam near't,
It was sae fine.

That, set him to a pint of ale,
An' either douce or merry tale,
Or rhymes an' sangs he'd made himsel,
Or witty catches,
'Tween Inverness and Tiviotdale,
He had few matches.

Then up I gat, an' swoor an aith,
Tho' I should pawn my pleugh an' graith,
Or die a cadger pownie's death,
At some dyke-back,
A pint an' gill I'd gie them baith,
To hear your crack.

But, first an' foremost, I should tell,
Amaist as soon as I could spell,
I to the crambo-jingle fell,
Tho' rude an' rough,
Yet crooning to a body's sel,
Does weel eneugh.

I am nae Poet, in a sense,
But just a Rhymer, like, by chance,
An' hae to Learning nae pretence,
Yet, what the matter?

Margin glosses:
- put; tingling with delight
- asked
- genius
- sober
- harness
- hawker pony
- talk
- rhyming
- humming

Whene'er my Muse does on me glance,
      I jingle at her.

Your Critic-folk may cock their nose,
And say, 'How can you e'er propose,
'You wha ken hardly verse frae prose,
      'To make a sang?'
But, by your leaves, my learned foes,
      Ye're maybe wrang.

What's a' your jargon o' your Schools,
Your Latin names for horns an' stools;
If honest Nature made you fools,
      What sairs your Grammars?   serve
Ye'd better taen up spades and shools,   shovels
      Or knappin-hammers.   stone-breaking-

A set o' dull, conceited Hashes,   dunderheads
Confuse their brains in College-classes!
They gang in Stirks, and come out Asses,   steers
      Plain truth to speak;
An' syne they think to climb Parnassus   then
      By dint o' Greek!

Gie me ae spark o' Nature's fire,
That's a' the learning I desire;
Then tho' I drudge thro' dub an' mire   puddle
      At pleugh or cart,
My Muse, tho' hamely in attire,
      May touch the heart.

O for a spunk o' Allan's glee,   spark
Or Ferguson's,[1] the bauld an' slee,   bold

1. Ramsay's or Robert Fergusson's. Cf. p.112 – EDD.

Or bright Lapraik's, my friend to be,
If I can hit it!
learning   That would be lear eneugh for me,
If I could get it.

Now, Sir, if ye hae friends enow,
Tho' real friends I b'lieve are few,
full   Yet, if your catalogue be fou,
I'll   I'se no insist;
But gif ye want ae friend that's true,
I'm on your list.

brag   I winna blaw about mysel,
faults   As ill I like my fauts to tell;
But friends an' folks that wish me well,
praise   They sometimes roose me;
Tho' I maun own, as monie still
As far abuse me.

sometimes   There's ae wee faut they whyles lay to me,
God   I like the lasses—Gude forgie me!
coin   For monie a Plack they wheedle frae me,
At dance or fair;
Maybe some ither thing they gie me
They weel can spare.

But Mauchline Race or Mauchline Fair,
I should be proud to meet you there;
We'll   We'se gie ae night's discharge to care,
If we forgather,
swop   An' hae a swap o' rhymin-ware
Wi' ane anither.

The four-gill chap, we'se gar him clatter,
An' kirsen him wi' reekin water;
Syne we'll sit down an' tak our whitter,
   To chear our heart;
An' faith, we'se be acquainted better
   Before we part.

cup, we'll make
christen; steaming
Then; draught

Awa ye selfish, warly race,
Wha think that havins, sense, an' grace,
Ev'n love an' friendship, should give place
   To catch-the-plack!
I dinna like to see your face,
   Nor hear your crack.

worldly
manners
coining money

But ye whom social pleasure charms,
Whose hearts the tide of kindness warms,
Who hold your being on the terms,
   'Each aid the others,'
Come to my bowl, come to my arms,
   My friends, my brothers!

But to conclude my lang epistle,
As my auld pen's worn to the grissle;
Twa lines frae you wad gar me fissle,
   Who am, most fervent,
While I can either sing, or whissle,
   Your friend and servant.

make; tingle

TO THE SAME

newly driven
cattle low
smoke;
harrow

While new-ca'd kye rowte at the stake,
An' pownies reek in pleugh or braik,
This hour on e'enin's edge I take,
To own I'm debtor,
To honest-hearted, auld Lapraik,
For his kind letter.

Jaded
ridges; fields
nags

Forjesket sair, with weary legs,
Rattlin the corn out-owre the rigs,
Or dealing thro' amang the naigs
Their ten-hours bite,
awkward
My awkart Muse sair pleads and begs,
I would na write.

heedless,
exhausted
hussy

The tapetless, ramfeezl'd hizzie,
She's saft at best an' something lazy,
Quo' she, 'Ye ken we've been sae busy
'This month an' mair,
'That trouth, my head is grown right dizzie,
'An' something sair.'

weak; put
slack
screed
do not

Her dowff excuses pat me mad;
'Conscience,' says I, 'ye thowless jad!
'I'll write, an' that a hearty blaud,
'This vera night;
'So dinna ye affront your trade,
'But rhyme it right.

'Shall bauld Lapraik, the king o' hearts,
'Tho' mankind were a pack o' cartes,

'Roose you sae weel for your deserts,   *Praise*
        'In terms sae friendly,
'Yet ye'll neglect to shaw your parts   *show*
        'An' thank him kindly?'

Sae I gat paper in a blink,
An' down gaed stumpie in the ink:
Quoth I, 'Before I sleep a wink,
        'I vow I'll close it;
'An' if ye winna mak it clink,   *rhyme*
        'By Jove I'll prose it!'

Sae I've begun to scrawl, but whether
In rhyme, or prose, or baith thegither,
Or some hotch-potch that's rightly neither,
        Let time mak proof;
But I shall scribble down some blether   *nonsense*
        Just clean aff-loof.   *off-hand*

My worthy friend, ne'er grudge an' carp,
Tho' Fortune use you hard an' sharp;
Come, kittle up your moorland harp   *tickle*
        Wi' gleesome touch!
Ne'er mind how Fortune waft an' warp;   *weft*
        She's but a bitch.

She's gien me monie a jirt an' fleg,   *jerk; scare*
Sin' I could striddle owre a rig;   *straddle*
But, by the Lord, tho' I should beg
        Wi' lyart pow,   *grey head*
I'll laugh, an' sing, an' shake my leg,
        As lang's I dow!   *can*

Now comes the sax an' twentieth simmer,
<small>woods</small>   I've seen the bud upo' the timmer,
<small>jade</small>   Still persecuted by the limmer
      Frae year to year;
<small>fickle
woman</small>   But yet, despite the kittle kimmer,
      I, Rob, am here.

Do ye envy the city Gent,
<small>counter;
cheat</small>   Behint a kist to lie an' sklent,
Or purse-proud, big wi' cent. per cent.
<small>stomach</small>   An' muckle wame,
<small>small burgh</small>   In some bit Brugh to represent
<small>magistrate's</small>   A Bailie's name?

<small>haughty</small>   Or is't the paughty, feudal Thane,
<small>shirt</small>   Wi' ruffl'd sark an' glancing cane,
Wha thinks himsel nae sheep-shank bane,[1]
      But lordly stalks,
While caps an' bonnets aff are taen,
      As by he walks?

'O Thou wha gies us each guid gift!
<small>load</small>   'Gie me o' wit an' sense a lift,
'Then turn me, if Thou please, adrift,
      'Thro' Scotland wide;
<small>change
places</small>   'Wi' cits nor lairds I wadna shift,
      'In a' their pride!'

Were this the charter of our state,
'On pain o' hell be rich an' great,'
Damnation then would be our fate,
      Beyond remead;

1. Literally 'no sheep-leg bone,' i.e. no small beer. –EDD.

But, thanks to Heav'n, that's no the gate   way
        We learn our creed.

For thus the royal Mandate ran,
When first the human race began,
'The social, friendly, honest man,
        'Whate'er he be,
' 'Tis he fulfils great Nature's plan,
        'And none but he.'

O Mandate, glorious and divine!
The followers o' the ragged Nine,
Poor, thoughtless devils! yet may shine
        In glorious light,
While sordid sons o' Mammon's line
        Are dark as night.

Tho' here they scrape, an' squeeze, an' growl,
Their worthless neivefu' of a soul   handful
May in some future carcase howl,
        The forest's fright;
Or in some day-detesting owl
        May shun the light.

Then may Lapraik and Burns arise,
To reach their native, kindred skies,
And sing their pleasures, hopes an' joys,
        In some mild sphere,
Still closer knit in friendship's ties
        Each passing year!

TO WILLIAM SIMPSON,
OCHILTREE

I gat your letter, winsome Willie;
heartily   Wi' gratefu' heart I thank you brawlie;
Tho' I maun say't, I wad be silly,
         An' unco vain,
fellow   Should I believe, my coaxin billie,
         Your flatterin strain.

I'll   But I'se believe ye kindly meant it,
loath   I sud be laith to think ye hinted
sideways
squinted   Ironic satire, sidelins sklented
         On my poor Musie;
wheedling   Tho' in sic phraisin terms ye've penn'd it,
         I scarce excuse ye.

whirl   My senses wad be in a creel,
climb   Should I but dare a hope to speel,
Wi' Allan, or wi' Gilbertfield,
         The braes o' fame;
lawyer-chap   Or Ferguson,[1] the writer-chiel,
         A deathless name.

(O Ferguson! thy glorious parts
Ill suited law's dry, musty arts!
whinstone   My curse upon your whunstane hearts,
         Ye Enbrugh Gentry!
The tythe o' what ye waste at cartes
Would have
stored   Wad stow'd his pantry!)

    1. The poets Ramsay, William Hamilton and Robert Fergusson.
– EDD.

To William Simpson, Ochiltree

Yet when a tale comes i' my head,
Or lasses gie my heart a screed,   *rent*
As whiles they're like to be my dead,   *sometimes;*
             (O sad disease!)   *death*
I kittle up my rustic reed;   *tickle*
             It gies me ease.

Auld Coila,[1] now, may fidge fu' fain,   *tingle with*
She's gotten Poets o' her ain,   *delight*
Chiels wha their chanters winna hain,   *spare*
             But tune their lays,
Till echoes a' resound again
             Her weel-sung praise.

Nae Poet thought her worth his while,
To set her name in measur'd style;
She lay like some unkend-of isle
             Beside New Holland,
Or whare wild-meeting oceans boil
             Besouth Magellan.

Ramsay an' famous Ferguson
Gied Forth an' Tay a lift aboon;
Yarrow an' Tweed, to monie a tune,   *up*
             Owre Scotland rings,
While Irwin, Lugar, Ayr, an' Doon,
             Naebody sings.

Th' Illissus, Tiber, Thames, an' Seine,
Glide sweet in monie a tunefu' line;
But, Willie, set your fit to mine,   *foot*
             An' cock your crest,
We'll gar our streams an' burnies shine   *make*
             Up wi' the best.

1. Kyle in Ayrshire. – EDD.

To William Simpson, Ochiltree

We'll sing auld Coila's plains an' fells,
Her moors red-brown wi' heather bells,
Her banks an' braes, her dens an' dells,
        Whare glorious Wallace

bore off the prize   Aft bure the gree, as story tells,
        Frae Suthron billies.

At Wallace' name, what Scottish blood
But boils up in a spring-tide flood!
Oft have our fearless fathers strode
        By Wallace' side,

-wet   Still pressing onward, red-wat shod,
        Or glorious dy'd!

hollows   O sweet are Coila's haughs an' woods,
linnets   When lintwhites chant amang the buds,
sporting; gambols   And jinkin hares, in amorous whids,
        Their loves enjoy,
wood-pigeon   While thro' the braes the cushat croods
        With wailfu' cry!

Ev'n winter bleak has charms to me
When winds rave thro' the naked tree;
Or frosts on hills of Ochiltree
        Are hoary gray;
Or blinding drifts wild-furious flee,
        Dark'ning the day!

O Nature! a' thy shews an' forms
To feeling, pensive hearts hae charms!
Whether the Summer kindly warms,
        Wi' life an' light,
Or Winter howls, in gusty storms,
        The lang, dark night!

To William Simpson, Ochiltree

The Muse, nae Poet ever fand her,   found
Till by himsel he learn'd to wander,
Adown some trotting burn's meander,
                    An' no think lang;
O sweet, to stray an' pensive ponder
                    A heart-felt sang!

The warly race may drudge an' drive,   worldly
Hog-shouther, jundie, stretch an' strive,   push; jostle
Let me fair Nature's face descrive,
                    And I, wi' pleasure,
Shall let the busy, grumbling hive
                    Bum owre their treasure.

Fareweel, 'my rhyme-composing brither!'
We've been owre lang unkenn'd to ither: too long
Now let us lay our heads thegither,   unknown
                    In love fraternal:
May Envy wallop in a tether,
                    Black fiend, infernal!

While Highlandmen hate tolls an' taxes;
While moorlan herds like guid, fat braxies;   dead sheep
While Terra Firma, on her axis,
                    Diurnal turns,
Count on a friend, in faith an' practice,
                    In Robert Burns.

*   *   *   *

SONG

TUNE, *Corn rigs are bonie*

I

It was upon a Lammas night,
    When corn rigs are bonie,
Beneath the moon's unclouded light,
    I held awa to Annie:
The time flew by, wi' tentless heed,
    Till, 'tween the late and early;
Wi' sma' persuasion she agreed,
    To see me thro' the barley.

II

The sky was blue, the wind was still,
    The moon was shining clearly;
I set her down, wi' right good will,
    Amang the rigs o' barley:
I ken't her heart was a' my ain;
    I lov'd her most sincerely;
I kiss'd her owre and owre again,
    Amang the rigs o' barley.

III

I lock'd her in my fond embrace;
    Her heart was beating rarely:
My blessings on that happy place,
    Amang the rigs o' barley!
But by the moon and stars so bright,
    That shone that hour so clearly!
She ay shall bless that happy night,
    Amang the rigs o' barley.

fields

careless

knew; own

Song

IV

I hae been blythe wi' comrades dear;
　I hae been merry drinking;
I hae been joyfu' gath'rin gear;　　　　　money-
　I hae been happy thinking:　　　　　　　making
But a' the pleasures e'er I saw,
　Tho' three times doubl'd fairly,
That happy night was worth them a',
　Amang the rigs o' barley.

CHORUS

Corn rigs, an' barley rigs,
　An' corn rigs are bonie:
I'll ne'er forget that happy night,
　Amang the rigs wi' Annie.

A BARD'S EPITAPH

Is there a whim-inspired fool,
Owre fast for thought, owre hot for rule,

Too
shy; cringe
Owre blate to seek, owre proud to snool,
       Let him draw near;
woe
And owre this grassy heap sing dool,
       And drap a tear.

Is there a Bard of rustic song,
Who, noteless, steals the crowds among,
That weekly this area throng,
       O, pass not by!
But, with a frater-feeling strong,
       Here, heave a sigh.

Is there a man, whose judgment clear
Can others teach the course to steer,
Yet runs, himself, life's mad career,
       Wild as the wave;
Here pause – and, through the starting tear,
       Survey this grave.

The poor Inhabitant below
Was quick to learn and wise to know,
And keenly felt the friendly glow,
       And softer flame;
But thoughtless follies laid him low,
       And stain'd his name!

A Bard's Epitaph

Reader, attend – whether thy soul
Soars fancy's flights beyond the pole,
Or darkling grubs this earthly hole,
          In low pursuit;
Know, prudent, cautious, self-controul
          Is Wisdom's root.

Poems in the Edinburgh Edition, 1787

DEATH AND DOCTOR HORNBOOK

A TRUE STORY

Some books are lies frae end to end,
And some great lies were never penn'd:
Ev'n Ministers they hae been kenn'd,   known
           In holy rapture,
A rousing whid, at times, to vend,   lie; vent
           And nail't wi' Scripture.

But this that I am gaun to tell,
Which lately on a night befel,
Is just as true's the Deil's in hell
           Or Dublin city:
That e'er he nearer comes oursel
           'S a muckle pity.   great

The Clachan yill had made me canty,   village ale; jolly
I was na fou, but just had plenty;   drunk
I stacher'd whyles, but yet took tent ay   staggered now and then; care
           To free the ditches;   clear
An' hillocks, stanes, an' bushes kenn'd ay   knew
           Frae ghaists an' witches.

The rising Moon began to glowr
The distant Cumnock hills out-owre: away over
To count her horns, wi' a' my pow'r
           I set mysel;
But whether she had three or four,
           I cou'd na tell.

I was come round about the hill,
And todlin down on Willie's mill,

Setting my staff wi' a' my skill,

steady   To keep me sicker;

at times Tho' leeward whyles, against my will,

run   I took a bicker.

meet I there wi' *Something* does forgather,

put;
doubt That pat me in an eerie swither;

over one
shoulder An awfu' scythe, out-owre ae shouther,

                Clear-dangling, hang;

three-
pronged A three-tae'd leister on the ither
fish-spear

                Lay, large an' lang.

Its stature seem'd lang Scotch ells twa,

The queerest shape that e'er I saw,

devil; belly; For fient a wame it had ava;
at all

                And then its shanks,

They were as thin, as sharp an' sma'

wooden
bridle   As cheeks o' branks.

mowing 'Guid-een,' quo' I; 'Friend! hae ye been mawin,

sowing 'When ither folk are busy sawin?'[1]

stand It seem'd to mak a kind o' stan',

                But naething spak;

where are ye At length, says I, 'Friend, whare ye gaun,
going

                'Will ye go back?'

hollow It spak right howe – 'My name is Death,

scared 'But be na' fley'd.' – Quoth I, 'Guid faith,

'Ye're maybe come to stap my breath;

heed; fellow   'But tent me, billie;

advise; 'I red ye weel, tak care o' skaith,
harm

large knife   'See, there's a gully!'

1. This rencounter happened in seed-time, 1785.

'Gudeman,' quo' he, 'put up your whittle,   blade
'I'm no design'd to try its mettle;
'But if I did, I wad be kittle   inclined
           'To be mislear'd,   mischievous
'I wad na mind it, no that spittle
           'Out-owre my beard.'

'Weel, weel!' says I, 'a bargain be't;
'Come, gie's your hand, an' sae we're gree't: agreed
'We'll ease our shanks an' tak a seat,
           'Come, gies your news;
'This while[1] ye hae been mony a gate,   road
           'At mony a house.'

'Ay, ay!' quo' he, an' shook his head,
'It's e'en a lang, lang time indeed
'Sin I began to nick the thread,   cut
           'An' choke the breath:
'Folk maun do something for their bread,
           'An' sae maun Death.

'Sax thousand years are near hand fled   well-nigh
'Sin' I was to the butching bred,
'An' mony a scheme in vain's been laid,
           'To stap or scar me;   stop; scare
'Till ane Hornbook's[2] ta'en up the trade,
           'An' faith, he'll waur me.   worst

'Ye ken Jock Hornbook i' the Clachan,   village
'Deil mak his king's-hood in a spleuchan!   stomach
                                     into a tobacco-pouch

1. An epidemical fever was then raging in that country.
2. This gentleman, Dr Hornbook, is, professionally, a brother of the sovereign Order of the Ferula; but, by intuition and inspiration, is at once an Apothecary, Surgeon, and Physician.

'He's grown sae weel acquaint wi' Buchan,[1]
    'And ither chaps,
children 'The weans haud out their fingers laughin,
poke   'An' pouk my hips.

'See, here's a scythe, an' there's a dart,
'They hae pierc'd mony a gallant heart;
'But Doctor Hornbook, wi' his art
    'And cursed skill,
'Has made them baith no worth a fart,
The devil a   'Damn'd haet they'll kill!
one

''Twas but yestreen, nae farther gaen,
'I threw a noble throw at ane;
'Wi' less, I'm sure, I've hundreds slain;
    'But deil-ma-care!
rattle; bone 'It just play'd dirl on the bane,
no more   'But did nae mair.

'Hornbook was by, wi' ready art,
'An' had sae fortify'd the part,
'That when I looked to my dart,
    'It was sae blunt,
Devil a bit 'Fient haet o't wad hae pierc'd the heart
cabbage-   'Of a kail-runt.
stalk

'I drew my scythe in sic a fury,
almost 'I nearhand cowpit wi' my hurry,
tumbled 'But yet the bauld Apothecary
    'Withstood the shock;
'I might as weel hae try'd a quarry
    'O' hard whin-rock.

1. Buchan's Domestic Medicine.

'Ev'n them he canna get attended,
'Altho' their face he ne'er had kend it,   known
'Just shit in a kail-blade and send it,   cabbage-leaf
                'As soon's he smells't,
'Baith their disease, and what will mend it,
                'At once he tells't.

'And then a' doctor's saws and whittles,   knives
'Of a' dimensions, shapes, an' mettles,
'A' kinds o' boxes, mugs, an' bottles,
                'He's sure to hae;
'Their Latin names as fast he rattles
           'As A B C.

'Calces o' fossils, earth, and trees;
'True Sal-marinum o' the seas;
'The Farina of beans and pease,
             'He has't in plenty;
'Aqua-fontis, what you please,
             'He can content ye.

'Forbye some new, uncommon weapons,   Besides
'Urinus Spiritus of capons;
'Or Mite-horn shavings, filings, scrapings,
             'Distill'd *per se*;
'Sal-alkali o' Midge-tail-Clippings,
             'And mony mae.'   many more

'Waes me for Johnny Ged's Hole[1] now,'
Quoth I, 'if that thae news be true!   these
'His braw calf-ward whare gowans grew,   fine pasture
             'Sae white and bonie,
'Nae doubt they'll rive it wi' the plew;   split; plough
             'They'll ruin Johnie!'

1. The grave-digger.

The creature grain'd an eldritch laugh,
And says 'Ye needna yoke the pleugh,
'Kirk-yards will soon be till'd eneugh,
                    'Tak ye nae fear:
'They'll a' be trench'd wi mony a sheugh,
                    'In twa-three year.

'Whare I kill'd ane, a fair strae-death,
'By loss o' blood, or want o' breath,
'This night I'm free to tak my aith,
                    'That Hornbook's skill
'Has clad a score i' their last claith,
                    'By drap and pill.

'An honest Wabster to his trade,
'Whase wife's twa nieves were scarce weel-bred,
'Gat tippence-worth to mend her head,
                    'When it was sair;
'The wife slade cannie to her bed,
                    'But ne'er spak mair.

'A countra Laird had ta'en the batts,
'Or some curmurring in his guts,
'His only son for Hornbook sets,
                    'An' pays him well.
'The lad, for twa guid gimmer-pets,
                    'Was Laird himsel.

'A bonie lass, ye kend her name,
'Some ill-brewn drink had hov'd her wame;
'She trusts hersel, to hide the shame,
                    'In Hornbook's care;
'Horn sent her aff to her lang hame,
                    'To hide it there.

128

Marginal glosses:
groaned; weird
ditch
in a straw-bed
oath
cloth
weaver
fists
aching
crept quietly
colic
rumbling
pet-ewes
swelled; belly
long home

'That's just a swatch o' Hornbook's way, sample
'Thus goes he on from day to day,
'Thus does he poison, kill, an' slay,
    'An's weel paid for't;
'Yet stops me o' my lawfu' prey,
     'Wi' his damn'd dirt!

'But hark! I'll tell you of a plot,
'Tho' dinna ye be speakin o't;
'I'll nail the self-conceited Sot,
    'As dead's a herrin:
'Niest time we meet, I'll wad a groat, Next; wager
     'He gets his fairin!' deserts

But just as he began to tell,
The auld kirk-hammer strak the bell
Some wee short hour ayont the twal, beyond;
     Which rais'd us baith: twelve
I took the way that pleas'd mysel,
     And sae did Death.

THE BRIGS OF AYR

A Poem

INSCRIBED TO JOHN BALLANTINE, ESQ. AYR

* * * *

'Twas when the stacks get on their winter-hap, *(wrap)*
And thack and rape secure the toil-won crap; *(thatch; rope; crop)*
Potatoe-bings are snugged up frae skaith *(heaps; damage)*
Of coming Winter's biting, frosty breath;
The bees rejoicing o'er their summer toils,
Unnumber'd buds an' flowers' delicious spoils,
Seal'd up with frugal care in massive waxen piles,
Are doom'd by Man, that tyrant o'er the weak,
The death o' devils, smoor'd wi' brimstone reek: *(smothered; smoke)*
The thund'ring guns are heard on ev'ry side,
The wounded coveys, reeling, scatter wide;
The feather'd field-mates, bound by Nature's tie,
Sires, mothers, children, in one carnage lie:
(What warm, poetic heart but inly bleeds,
And execrates man's savage, ruthless deeds!)
Nae mair the flow'r in field or meadow springs;
Nae mair the grove with airy concert rings,
Except perhaps the Robin's whistling glee,
Proud o' the height o' some bit half-lang tree: *(small half-sized)*
The hoary morns precede the sunny days,
Mild, calm, serene, wide-spreads the noontide
    blaze,
While thick the gossamour waves wanton in the
    . rays.

'Twas in that season, when a simple Bard,
Unknown and poor, simplicity's reward,

The Brigs of Ayr

Ae night, within the ancient brugh of Ayr,   burgh
By whim inspir'd, or haply prest wi' care,
He left his bed, and took his wayward rout,
And down by Simpson's[1] wheel'd the left about:
(Whether impell'd by all-directing Fate,
To witness what I after shall narrate;
Or whether, rapt in meditation high,
He wander'd out he knew not where nor why)
The drowsy Dungeon-clock[2] had number'd two,
And Wallace Tow'r[2] had sworn the fact was true:
The tide-swoln Firth, with sullen-sounding roar,
Through the still night dash'd hoarse along the
         shore:
All else was hush'd as Nature's closed e'e;
The silent moon shone high o'er tow'r and tree:
The chilly Frost, beneath the silver beam,
Crept, gently-crusting, o'er the glittering stream. –

When, lo! on either hand the list'ning Bard,
The clanging sugh of whistling wings is heard;   sough
Two dusky forms dart thro' the midnight air,
Swift as the Gos[3] drives on the wheeling hare;
Ane on th' Auld Brig his airy shape uprears,
The ither flutters o'er the rising piers;
Our warlock Rhymer instantly descry'd   wizard
The Sprites that owre the Brigs of Ayr preside.
(That Bards are second-sighted is nae joke,
And ken the lingo of the sp'ritual folk;
Fays, Spunkies, Kelpies, a', they can explain them,   will-o'-the-
                                                        wisps; water-
And ev'n the vera deils they brawly ken them).   demons
                                                        known them
                                                        well

1. A noted tavern at the *Auld Brig* end.
2. The two steeples.   3. The goshawk, or falcon.

Auld Brig appear'd of ancient Pictish race,
The vera wrinkles Gothic in his face:
wrestled He seem'd as he wi' Time had warstl'd lang,
toughly
stubborn Yet, teughly doure, he bade an unco bang.
stood up to New Brig was buskit in a braw, new coat,
That he, at Lon'on, frae ane Adams, got;
In's hand five taper staves as smooth's a bead,
rings Wi' virls an' whirlygigums at the head.
The Goth was stalking round with anxious search,
Spying the time-worn flaws in ev'ry arch;
It chanc'd his new-come neebor took his e'e,
And e'en a vex'd and angry heart had he!
spiteful Wi' thieveless sneer to see his modish mien,
He, down the water, gies him this guid-een –

AULD BRIG

'no small I doubt na, frien', ye'll think ye're nae sheep-shank,
beer'
stretched Ance ye were streekit owre frae bank to bank!
across
when But gin ye be a brig as auld as me,
Tho' faith, that date I doubt, ye'll never see;
wager a There'll be, if that day come, I'll wad a boddle,
farthing Some fewer whigmeleeries in your noddle.

NEW BRIG

manners Auld Vandal, ye but show your little mense,
Just much about it wi' your scanty sense;
Will your poor, narrow foot-path of a street,
Where twa wheel-barrows tremble when they meet,
Your ruin'd, formless bulk o' stane an' lime,
Compare wi' bonie Brigs o' modern time?
There's men of taste wou'd tak the Ducat-stream,[1]

1. A noted ford, just above the Auld Brig.

Tho' they should cast the vera sark and swim,   shirt
E'er they would grate their feelings wi' the view
Of sic an ugly, Gothic hulk as you.

AULD BRIG

Conceited gowk! puff'd up wi' windy pride!   cuckoo
This mony a year I've stood the flood an' tide;
And tho' wi' crazy eild I'm sair forfairn,   eld;
                                              worn out
I'll be a Brig when ye're a shapeless cairn!
As yet ye little ken about the matter,
But twa-three winters will inform ye better.
When heavy, dark, continued, a'-day rains,
Wi' deepening deluges o'erflow the plains;
When from the hills where springs the brawling Coil,
Or stately Lugar's mossy fountains boil,
Or where the Greenock winds his moorland course,
Or haunted Garpal[1] draws his feeble source,
Arous'd by blustering winds an' spotting thowes,   thaws
In mony a torrent down the snaw-broo rowes;   melted snow
                                               rolls
While crashing ice, borne on the roaring speat,   spate
Sweeps dams, an' mills, an' brigs, a' to the gate;   away
And from Glenbuck,[2] down to the Ratton-key,[3]
Auld Ayr is just one lengthen'd, tumbling sea;
Then down ye'll hurl, deil nor ye never rise!   crash
And dash the gumlie jaups up to the pouring skies.   muddy
                                                      splashes
A lesson sadly teaching, to your cost,
That Architecture's noble art is lost!

1. The banks of Garpal Water is one of the few places in the West
of Scotland where those fancy-scaring beings, known by the name
of *Ghaists*, still continue pertinaciously to inhabit.
2. The source of the river of Ayr.
3. A small landing-place above the large key.

NEW BRIG

Fine architecture, trowth, I needs must say't o't!
lost the way The Lord be thankit that we've tint the gate o't!
Gaunt, ghastly, ghaist-alluring edifices,
Hanging with threat'ning jut, like precipices;
O'er-arching, mouldy, gloom-inspiring coves,
Supporting roofs, fantastic, stony groves:
Windows and doors in nameless sculptures drest,
With order, symmetry, or taste unblest;
Forms like some bedlam Statuary's dream,
The craz'd creations of misguided whim;
Forms might be worshipp'd on the bended knee, ⎫
And still the second dread command be free, ⎬
Their likeness is not found on earth, in air, or sea. ⎭
Mansions that would disgrace the building-taste
Of any mason reptile, bird, or beast;
stupid Fit only for a doited Monkish race,
Or frosty maids forsworn the dear embrace,
fools Or Cuifs of later times, wha held the notion,
That sullen gloom was sterling, true devotion:
Fancies that our guid Brugh denies protection,
And soon may they expire, unblest with resurrection!

AULD BRIG

contempor-aries O ye, my dear-remember'd, ancient yealings,
Were ye but here to share my wounded feelings!
provosts; magistrate Ye worthy Proveses, an' mony a Bailie,
Wha in the paths o' righteousness did toil ay;
sedate Ye dainty Deacons, an' ye douce Conveeners,
causeway- To whom our moderns are but causey-cleaners;
Ye godly Councils, wha hae blest this town;
Ye godly Brethren o' the sacred gown,

134

Wha meekly gae your hurdies to the smiters;   *buttocks*
And (what would now be strange) ye godly Writers;   *Lawyers*
A' ye douce folk I've borne aboon the broo,   *over; flood*
Were ye but here, what would ye say or do!
How would your spirits groan in deep vexation,
To see each melancholy alteration;
And agonizing, curse the time and place
When ye begat the base, degen'rate race!
Nae langer Rev'rend Men, their country's glory,
In plain, braid Scots hold forth a plain, braid story: *broad*
Nae langer thrifty Citizens, an' douce,
Meet owre a pint or in the Council-house;
But staumrel, corky-headed, graceless Gentry,   *half-witted*
The herryment and ruin of the country;   *harrying*
Men, three-parts made by Taylors and by Barbers,
Wha waste your weel-hain'd gear on damn'd new   *well-saved*
    Brigs and Harbours!   *wealth*

NEW BRIG

Now haud you there! for faith ye've said enough,   *hold*
And muckle mair than ye can mak to through.   *much more; make good*
As for your Priesthood, I shall say but little,
Corbies and Clergy are a shot right kittle: *Ravens; ticklish lot*
But, under favor o' your langer beard,
Abuse o' Magistrates might weel be spar'd:
To liken them to your auld-warld squad,
I must needs say, comparisons are odd.
In Ayr, Wag-wits nae mair can have a handle
To mouth 'A Citizen,' a term o' scandal:
Nae mair the Council waddles down the street,
In all the pomp of ignorant conceit;
Men wha grew wise priggin owre hops an' raisins,   *haggling*
Or gather'd lib'ral views in Bonds and Seisins.   *deeds*

If haply Knowledge, on a random tramp,
threatened Had shor'd them with a glimmer of his lamp,
And would to Common-sense for once betray'd
them,
Plain, dull Stupidity stept kindly in to aid them.

* * * *

ADDRESS TO THE UNCO GUID,

OR THE RIGIDLY RIGHTEOUS

> *My son, these maxims make a rule,*
> *And lump them ay thegither;*   together
> The Rigid Righteous *is a fool,*
> The Rigid Wise *anither:*
> *The cleanest corn that e'er was dight*   sifted
> *May hae some pyles o' caff in;*   chaff
> *So ne'er a fellow-creature slight*
> *For random fits o' daffin.*   larking

SOLOMON – *Eccles.* ch. vii. ver. 16.

I

O ye wha are sae guid yoursel,
  Sae pious and sae holy,
Ye've nought to do but mark and tell
  Your Neebours' fauts and folly!   faults
Whase life is like a weel-gaun mill,   well-going
  Supply'd wi' store o' water,
The heapet happer's ebbing still,   hopper
  An' still the clap plays clatter.

II

Hear me, ye venerable Core,   company
  As counsel for poor mortals,
That frequent pass douce Wisdom's door   sober
  For glaikit Folly's portals;   giddy
I, for their thoughtless, careless sakes,
  Would here propone defences,   put forward
Their donsie tricks, their black mistakes,   unlucky
  Their failings and mischances.

III

Ye see your state wi' theirs compar'd,
    And shudder at the niffer,
But cast a moment's fair regard,
    What maks the mighty differ;
Discount what scant occasion gave,
    That purity ye pride in,
And (what's aft mair than a' the lave)
    Your better art o' hiding.

exchange (margin)
rest (margin)

IV

Think, when your castigated pulse
    Gies now and then a wallop,
What ragings must his veins convulse,
    That still eternal gallop:
Wi' wind and tide fair i' your tail,
    Right on ye scud your sea-way;
But in the teeth o' baith to sail,
    It maks an unco leeway.

V

See Social-life and Glee sit down,
    All joyous and unthinking,
Till, quite transmugrify'd, they're grown
    Debauchery and Drinking:
O would they stay to calculate
    Th' eternal consequences;
Or your more dreaded hell to state,
    Damnation of expences!

VI

Ye high, exalted, virtuous Dames,
    Ty'd up in godly laces,

Before ye gie poor Frailty names,
   Suppose a change o' cases;
A dear-lov'd lad, convenience snug,
   A treacherous inclination –
But, let me whisper i' your lug,   ear
   Ye're aiblins nae temptation.   maybe

VII

Then gently scan your brother Man,
   Still gentler sister Woman;
Tho' they may gang a kennin wrang,   little
   To step aside is human:
One point must still be greatly dark,
   The moving *Why* they do it;
And just as lamely can ye mark,
   How far perhaps they rue it.

VIII

Who made the heart, 'tis *He* alone
   Decidedly can try us,
He knows each chord its various tone,
   Each spring its various bias:
Then at the balance let's be mute,
   We never can adjust it;
What's *done* we partly may compute,
   But know not what's *resisted*.

A WINTER NIGHT

Poor naked wretches, wheresoe'er you are,
That bide the pelting of this pityless storm!
How shall your houseless heads, and unfed sides,
Your loop'd and window'd raggedness, defend you
From seasons such as these –

SHAKESPEARE

hard   When biting Boreas, fell and doure,
     Sharp shivers thro' the leafless bow'r;
stare   When Phœbus gies a short-liv'd glow'r,
sky   Far south the lift,
     Dim-dark'ning thro' the flaky show'r,
       Or whirling drift.

     Ae night the Storm the steeples rocked,
     Poor Labour sweet in sleep was locked,
     While burns, wi' snawy wreeths up-choked,
       Wild-eddying swirl,
vomited   Or thro' the mining outlet bocked,
       Down headlong hurl.

windows   List'ning, the doors an' winnocks rattle,
shivering   I thought me on the ourie cattle,
onset   Or silly sheep, wha bide this brattle
       O' winter war,
-sinking, scramble   And thro the drift, deep-lairing, sprattle,
       Beneath a scar.

Each hopping   Ilk happing bird, wee, helpless thing!
     That, in the merry months o' spring,
     Delighted me to hear thee sing,
       What comes o' thee?

A Winter Night

Whare wilt thou cow'r thy chittering wing,   trembling
        An' close thy e'e?

Ev'n you on murd'ring errands toil'd,
Lone from your savage homes exil'd,
The blood-stain'd roost, and sheep-cote spoil'd,
        My heart forgets,
While pityless the tempest wild
        Sore on you beats.

*   *   *   *

TO A HAGGIS

jolly

Fair fa' your honest, sonsie face,
Great Chieftain o' the Puddin-race!
Aboon them a' ye tak your place,

Paunch;
small guts

Painch, tripe, or thairm:

worthy

Weel are ye wordy of a grace
As lang's my arm.

The groaning trencher there ye fill,

buttocks

Your hurdies like a distant hill,
Your pin wad help to mend a mill
In time o' need,
While thro' your pores the dews distil
Like amber bead.

clean

His knife see Rustic-labour dight,

skill

An' cut you up wi' ready slight,
Trenching your gushing entrails bright
Like onie ditch;
And then, O what a glorious sight,

-smoking

Warm-reekin, rich!

horn-spoon

Then, horn for horn they stretch an' strive,
Deil tak the hindmost, on they drive,

well-swelled
stomachs
by-and-by

Till a' their weel-swall'd kytes belyve
Are bent like drums;

almost;
burst

Then auld Guidman, maist like to rive,
Bethankit hums.

Is there that owre his French *ragout*,

surfeit

Or *olio* that wad staw a sow,

142

Or *fricassee* wad mak her spew
            Wi' perfect sconner,   disgust
Looks down wi' sneering, scornfu' view
            On sic a dinner?

Poor devil! see him owre his trash,
As feckless as a wither'd rash,   feeble; rush
His spindle shank a guid whip-lash,
            His nieve a nit;   fist; nut
Thro' bluidy flood or field to dash,
            O how unfit!

But mark the Rustic, haggis-fed,
The trembling earth resounds his tread,
Clap in his walie nieve a blade,   ample
            He'll mak it whissle;
An' legs, an' arms, an' heads will sned,   top off
            Like taps o' thrissle.   tops of thistle

Ye Pow'rs wha mak mankind your care,
And dish them out their bill o' fare,
Auld Scotland wants nae skinking ware,   watery splashes;
            That jaups in luggies;   wooden porringers
But, if ye wish her gratefu' prayer,
            Gie her a Haggis!

MY NANIE, O

I

Behind yon hills where Lugar flows,
  'Mang moors an' mosses many, O,
The wintry sun the day has clos'd,
  And I'll awa to Nanie, O.

II

western;
shrill
murky

The westlin wind blaws loud an' shill;
  The night's baith mirk and rainy O;
But I'll get my plaid an' out I'll steal,
  An' owre the hill to Nanie, O.

III

My Nanie's charming, sweet an' young;
  Nae artfu' wiles to win ye, O:
May ill befa' the flattering tongue
  That wad beguile my Nanie, O.

IV

Her face is fair, her heart is true,
  As spotless as she's bonie, O;
The op'ning gowan, wat wi' dew,
  Nae purer is than Nanie, O.

V

A country lad is my degree,
  An' few there be that ken me, O;
But what care I how few they be,
  I'm welcome ay to Nanie, O.

VI

My riches a's my penny-fee,   is all; wages
   An' I maun guide it cannie, O;   carefully
But warl's gear ne'er troubles me,   world's
   My thoughts are a', my Nanie, O. wealth

VII

Our auld Guidman delights to view
   His sheep an' kye thrive bonie, O;   kine
But I'm as blythe that hauds his pleugh, holds;
   An' has nae care but Nanie, O.   plough

VIII

Come weel come woe, I care na by,   do not care
   I'll tak what Heav'n will sen' me, O:
Nae ither care in life have I,
   But live, an' love my Nanie, O.

GREEN GROW THE RASHES

A Fragment

CHORUS

Green grow the rashes, O;
Green grow the rashes, O;
The sweetest hours that e'er I spent,
Are spent amang the lasses, O.

I

There's nought but care on ev'ry han',
    In every hour that passes, O:
What signifies the life o' man,
    An' 'twere na for the lasses, O.

II

worldly   The warly race may riches chase,
    An' riches still may fly them O;
An' tho' at last they catch them fast,
    Their hearts can ne'er enjoy them, O.

III

quiet   But gie me a cannie hour at e'en,
    My arms about my Dearie, O;
An' warly cares, an' warly men,
topsy-turvy   May a'gae tapsalteerie, O!

IV

sober   For you sae douse, ye sneer at this,
    Ye're nought but senseless asses, O:
world   The wisest Man the warl' e'er saw,
    He dearly lov'd the lasses, O.

V

Auld Nature swears, the lovely Dears
  Her noblest work she classes, O:
Her prentice han' she try'd on man,
  An' then she made the lasses, O.

Poems in the Edinburgh Edition, 1793

ELEGY ON CAPT. MATTHEW HENDERSON

A GENTLEMAN WHO HELD THE PATENT FOR HIS
HONOURS IMMEDIATELY FROM ALMIGHTY GOD!

But now his radiant course is run,
For Matthew's course was bright;
His soul was like the glorious sun,
A matchless Heavenly Light!

O Death! thou tyrant fell and bloody!
The meikle devil wi' a woodie   *great; halter*
Haurl thee hame to his black smiddie,   *Drag; smithy*
     O'er hurcheon hides,   *hedgehog*
And like stock-fish come o'er his studdie   *anvil*
     Wi' thy auld sides!

He's gane! he's gane! he's frae us torn,
The ae best fellow e'er was born!
Thee, Matthew, Nature's sel shall mourn   *self*
     By wood and wild,
Where, haply, Pity strays forlorn,
     Frae man exil'd.

Ye hills, near neebors o' the starns,   *stars*
That proudly cock your cresting cairns!
Ye cliffs, the haunts of sailing yearns,   *eagles*
     Where Echo slumbers!
Come join, ye Nature's sturdiest bairns,
     My wailing numbers!

Mourn, ilka grove the cushat kens!   *every; wood-pigeon*
Ye hazly shaws and briery dens!   *woods*

Capt. Matthew Henderson

rippling Ye burnies, wimplin down your glens,
tripping   Wi' toddlin din,
leaps Or foaming, strang, wi' hasty stens,
waterfall   Frae lin to lin.

Mourn, little harebells o'er the lee;
Ye stately foxgloves fair to see;
Ye woodbines hanging bonnilie,
       In scented bowers;
Ye roses on your thorny tree,
       The first o' flowers.

At dawn, when every grassy blade
Droops with a diamond at his head,
At even, when beans their fragrance shed,
       I' th' rustling gale,
hares
scampering Ye maukins whiddin thro' the glade,
       Come join my wail.

Mourn, ye wee songsters o' the wood;
crop Ye grouss that crap the heather bud;
cloud Ye curlews calling thro' a clud;
       Ye whistling plover;
partridge And mourn, ye whirring paitrick brood;
       He's gane for ever!

Mourn, sooty coots, and speckled teals;
Ye fisher herons, watching eels;
Ye duck and drake, wi' airy wheels
       Circling the lake;
Ye bitterns, till the quagmire reels,
Boom   Rair for his sake.

*   *   *   *

TAM O' SHANTER

A Tale

Of Brownyis and of Bogillis full is this buke.
GAWIN DOUGLAS

When chapman billies leave the street, · packman fellows
And drouthy neebors, neebors meet, · thirsty
As market-days are wearing late,
An' folk begin to tak the gate; · road
While we sit bousing at the nappy, · ale
An' getting fou and unco happy, · drunk; very
We think na on the lang Scots miles, · not
The mosses, waters, slaps, and styles, · gaps in walls
That lie between us and our hame,
Whare sits our sulky sullen dame,
Gathering her brows like gathering storm,
Nursing her wrath to keep it warm.

This truth fand honest Tam o' Shanter, · found
As he frae Ayr ae night did canter,
(Auld Ayr, wham ne'er a town surpasses,
For honest men and bonny lasses).

O Tam! had'st thou but been sae wise,
As ta'en thy ain wife Kate's advice! · taken; own
She tauld thee weel thou was a skellum, · rogue
A blethering, blustering, drunken blellum; · chattering; babbler
That frae November till October,
Ae market-day thou was nae sober;
That ilka melder, wi' the miller, · at every meal-grinding
Thou sat as lang as thou had siller; · money

That ev'ry naig was ca'd a shoe on, *nag that had a shoe driven on*
The smith and thee gat roaring fou on;
That at the Lord's house, even on Sunday,
Thou drank wi' Kirkton Jean till Monday.
She prophesied that, late or soon,
Thou would be found deep drown'd in Doon;
Or catch'd wi' warlocks in the mirk, *wizards; darkness*
By Alloway's auld haunted kirk.

Ah, gentle dames! it gars me greet, *makes; weep*
To think how mony counsels sweet,
How mony lengthen'd sage advices,
The husband frae the wife despises!

But to our tale: Ae market-night,
Tam had got planted unco right;
Fast by an ingle, bleezing finely,
Wi' reaming swats, that drank divinely; *frothing ale*
And at his elbow, Souter Johnny, *Cobbler*
His ancient, trusty, drouthy crony;
Tam lo'ed him like a vera brither;
They had been fou for weeks thegither.
The night drave on wi' sangs and clatter;
And ay the ale was growing better:
The landlady and Tam grew gracious,
Wi' favours, secret, sweet, and precious:
The Souter tauld his queerest stories;
The landlord's laugh was ready chorus:
The storm without might rair and rustle, *roar*
Tam did na mind the storm a whistle.

Care, mad to see a man sae happy,
E'en drown'd himsel amang the nappy:

As bees flee hame wi' lades o' treasure,   loads
The minutes wing'd their way wi' pleasure:
Kings may be blest, but Tam was glorious,
O'er a' the ills o' life victorious!

  But pleasures are like poppies spread,
You seize the flow'r, its bloom is shed;
Or like the snow falls in the river,
A moment white – then melts for ever;
Or like the borealis race,
That flit ere you can point their place;
Or like the rainbow's lovely form
Evanishing amid the storm. –
Nae man can tether time or tide;
The hour approaches Tam maun ride;
That hour, o' night's black arch the key-stane,
That dreary hour he mounts his beast in;
And sic a night he taks the road in,
As ne'er poor sinner was abroad in.

  The wind blew as 'twad blawn its last;   would have
The rattling showers rose on the blast;
The speedy gleams the darkness swallow'd;
Loud, deep, and lang, the thunder bellow'd:
That night, a child might understand,
The Deil had business on his hand.

  Weel mounted on his gray mare, Meg,
A better never lifted leg,
Tam skelpit on thro' dub and mire,   dashed;
                                     puddle
Despising wind, and rain, and fire;
Whiles holding fast his gude blue bonnet;   Now
Whiles crooning o'er some auld Scots sonnet;   song

staring   Whiles glowring round wi' prudent cares,
Lest bogles catch him unawares:
Kirk-Alloway was drawing nigh,
owls   Whare ghaists and houlets nightly cry. –

         By this time he was cross the ford,
smothered   Whare, in the snaw, the chapman smoor'd;
birches; big   And past the birks and meikle stane,
Whare drunken Charlie brak's neck-bane;
furze   And thro' the whins, and by the cairn,
Whare hunters fand the murder'd bairn;
And near the thorn, aboon the well,
Whare Mungo's mither hang'd hersel. –
Before him Doon pours all his floods;
The doubling storm roars thro' the woods;
The lightnings flash from pole to pole;
Near and more near the thunders roll:
When, glimmering thro' the groaning trees,
Kirk-Alloway seem'd in a bleeze;
every cranny   Thro' ilka bore the beams were glancing;
And loud resounded mirth and dancing. –

         Inspiring bold John Barleycorn!
What dangers thou canst make us scorn!
ale   Wi' tippeny, we fear nae evil;
whisky   Wi' usquabae, we'll face the devil! –
The swats sae ream'd in Tammie's noddle,
not; farthing   Fair play, he car'd na deils a boddle.
But Maggie stood right sair astonish'd,
Till, by the heel and hand admonish'd,
She ventur'd forward on the light;
wondrous   And, vow! Tam saw an unco sight!
Warlocks and witches in a dance;

Nae cotillion, brent new frae France,   brand
But hornpipes, jigs, strathspeys, and reels,
Put life and mettle in their heels.
A winnock-bunker in the east,   window-seat
There sat auld Nick, in shape o' beast;
A towzie tyke, black, grim, and large,   shaggy dog
To gie them music was his charge:
He screw'd the pipes and gart them skirl,   made
Till roof and rafters a' did dirl. –   rattle
Coffins stood round, like open presses,
That shaw'd the dead in their last dresses;
And by some devilish cantraip slight   weird trick
Each in its cauld hand held a light. –
By which heroic Tam was able
To note upon the haly table,
A murderer's banes in gibbet airns;   irons
Twa span-lang, wee, unchristen'd bairns;
A thief, new-cutted frae a rape,   rope
Wi' his last gasp his gab did gape;   mouth
Five tomahawks, wi' blude red-rusted;
Five scymitars, wi' murder crusted;
A garter, which a babe had strangled;
A knife, a father's throat had mangled,
Whom his ain son o' life bereft,
The grey hairs yet stack to the heft;   stuck; haft
Wi' mair o' horrible and awefu',
Which even to name wad be unlawfu'.

As Tammie glowr'd, amaz'd, and curious,   stared
The mirth and fun grew fast and furious:
The piper loud and louder blew;
The dancers quick and quicker flew;
They reel'd, they set, they cross'd, they cleekit,   joined hands

witch
sweated and
steamed
rags
Till ilka carlin swat and reekit,
And coost her duddies to the wark,

tripped;
shirt
And linket at it in her sark!

these
Now, Tam, O Tam! had thae been queans,
A' plump and strapping in their teens,

greasy
Their sarks, instead o' creeshie flannen,
Been snaw-white seventeen hunder linnen!

These
Thir breeks o' mine, my only pair,
That ance were plush, o' gude blue hair,

buttocks
I wad hae gi'en them off my hurdies,

lasses
For ae blink o' the bonie burdies!

But wither'd beldams, auld and droll,

Lean; wean
Rigwoodie hags wad spean a foal,

Leaping;
staff
Lowping and flinging on a crummock,
I wonder didna turn thy stomach.

well
But Tam kend what was what fu' brawlie,

choice
There was ae winsome wench and wawlie,

company
That night enlisted in the core,
(Lang after kend on Carrick shore;
For mony a beast to dead she shot,
And perish'd mony a bony boat.

much; barley
And shook baith meikle corn and bear,
And kept the country-side in fear).

short shift;
coarse cloth
Her cutty sark, o' Paisley harn,
That while a lassie she had worn,
In longitude tho' sorely scanty,

proud
It was her best, and she was vauntie. –
Ah! little kend thy reverend grannie,

bought
That sark she coft for her wee Nannie,
Wi' twa pund Scots ('twas a' her riches),
Wad ever grac'd a dance of witches!

But here my Muse her wing maun cour;   *stoop*
Sic flights are far beyond her pow'r;
To sing how Nannie lap and flang,   *leaped and*
(A souple jade she was, and strang),   *kicked*
And how Tam stood, like ane bewitch'd,
And thought his very een enrich'd;
Even Satan glowr'd, and fidg'd fu' fain,   *wriggled*
And hotch'd and blew wi' might and main: *with delight*
Till first ae caper, syne anither,   *jerked*
Tam tint his reason a' thegither,   *then*
And roars out, 'Weel done, Cutty-sark!'   *lost*
And in an instant all was dark:
And scarcely had he Maggie rallied,
When out the hellish legion sallied.

As bees bizz out wi' angry fyke,   *fret*
When plundering herds assail their byke;   *shepherds;*
As open pussie's mortal foes,   *hive*
When, pop! she starts before their nose;   *the hare's*
As eager runs the market-crowd,
When 'Catch the thief!' resounds aloud;
So Maggie runs, the witches follow,
Wi' mony an eldritch skreech and hollow.   *unearthly*
     yell

Ah, Tam! Ah, Tam! thou'll get thy fairin!   *deserts*
In hell they'll roast thee like a herrin!
In vain thy Kate awaits thy comin!
Kate soon will be a woefu' woman!
Now, do thy speedy utmost, Meg,
And win the key-stane[1] of the brig;
There at them thou thy tail may toss,

---

1. It is a well known fact that witches, or any evil spirits, have no power to follow a poor wight any farther than the middle of the

A running stream they dare na cross.
But ere the key-stane she could make,
devil   The fient a tail she had to shake!
For Nannie, far before the rest,
Hard upon noble Maggie prest,
intent   And flew at Tam wi' furious ettle;
But little wist she Maggie's mettle –
whole   Ae spring brought off her master hale,
But left behind her ain grey tail:
clutched   The carlin claught her by the rump,
And left poor Maggie scarce a stump.

Now, wha this tale o' truth shall read,
Ilk man and mother's son, take heed:
Whene'er to drink you are inclin'd,
Or cutty-sarks run in your mind,
Think, ye may buy the joys o'er dear,
Remember Tam o' Shanter's mare.

---

next running stream. – It may be proper likewise to mention to the
benighted traveller, that when he falls in with *bogles*, whatever
danger may be in his going forward, there is much more hazard in
turning back.

ON THE LATE CAPTAIN GROSE'S
PEREGRINATIONS THRO' SCOTLAND,

COLLECTING THE ANTIQUITIES OF THAT KINGDOM

Hear, Land o' Cakes, and brither Scots,
Frae Maidenkirk[1] to Johny Groats! –
If there's a hole in a' your coats,
    I rede you tent it: *advise; look to*
A chield's amang you, taking notes,   *fellow*
    And, faith, he'll prent it.   *print*

If in your bounds ye chance to light
Upon a fine, fat, fodgel wight,   *dumpy*
O' stature short, but genius bright,
    That's he, mark weel –
And wow! he has an unco slight   *skill*
    O' cauk and keel.   *chalk and ruddle*

By some auld, houlet-haunted biggin,[2]   *owl-; dwelling*
Or kirk deserted by its riggin,   *roof*
It's ten to ane ye'll find him snug in
    Some eldritch part,
Wi' deils, they say, Lord safe's! colleaguin   *save us*
    At some black art. –

Ilk ghaist that haunts auld ha' or chamer,   *Each; chamber*
Ye gipsy-gang that deal in glamor,
And you, deep-read in hell's black grammar,
    Warlocks and witches;
Ye'll quake at his conjuring hammer,
    Ye midnight bitches.

1. Kirkmaiden in Wigtownshire, the most southerly parish in
Scotland. – EDD.
2. *Vide* his Antiquities of Scotland.

It's tauld he was a sodger bred,
And ane wad rather fa'n than fled;
But now he's quat the spurtle-blade.
                              And dog-skin wallet,
And taen the – Antiquarian trade,
                              I think they call it.

would have;
fallen
quitted;
sword

He has a fouth o' auld nick-nackets:
Rusty airn caps and jingling jackets,[1]
Wad haud the Lothians three in tackets,
                              A towmont gude;
And parritch-pats, and auld saut-backets,
                              Before the Flood.

abundance
iron
Would keep;
shoenails
twelvemonth
porridge-
pots;
salt-boxes

Of Eve's first fire he has a cinder;
Auld Tubalcain's fire-shool and fender;
That which distinguished the gender
                              O' Balaam's ass;
A broom-stick o' the witch of Endor,
                              Weel shod wi' brass.

-shovel

Forbye, he'll shape you aff fu' gleg
The cut of Adam's philibeg;
The knife that nicket Abel's craig
                              He'll prove you fully,
It was a faulding jocteleg,
                              Or lang-kail gullie. –

Besides;
smartly
kilt
cut; throat
clasp knife
cabbage
knife

But wad ye see him in his glee,
For meikle glee and fun has he,
Then set him down, and twa or three
                              Gude fellows wi' him;

much

1. *Vide* his treatise on ancient armour and weapons.

And port, O port! shine thou a wee,
                    And THEN ye'll see him!

Now, by the Pow'rs o' Verse and Prose!
Thou art a dainty chield, O Grose! –
Whae'er o' thee shall ill suppose,
                    They sair misca' thee;
I'd take the rascal by the nose.
                    Wad say, Shame fa' thee.   befall

Poems from Various Sources

HOLY WILLIE'S PRAYER

And send the Godly in a pet to pray –
POPE

ARGUMENT

Holy Willie was a rather oldish batchelor Elder in the parish
of Mauchline [Ayrshire], & much & justly famed for that
polemical chattering which ends in tippling Orthodoxy, &
for that Spiritualized Bawdry which refines to Liquorish
Devotion. – In a Sessional process with a gentleman in
Mauchline, a Mr Gavin Hamilton, Holy Willie, & his priest,
father Auld, after full hearing in the Presbytery of Ayr, came
off but second best; owing partly to the oratorical powers of
Mr Robt Aiken, Mr Hamilton's Counsel; but chiefly to M.^r
Hamilton's being one of the most irreproachable & truly
respectable characters in the country. – On losing his Process,
the Muse overheard him at his devotions as follows –

O thou that in the heavens does dwell!
Wha, as it pleases best thysel,
Sends ane to heaven & ten to hell,
　　　　　A' for thy glory!
And no for ony gude or ill
　　　　　They've done before thee.

I bless & praise thy matchless might,
When thousands thou has left in night,
That I am here before thy sight,
　　　　　For gifts & grace,
A burning & a shining light
　　　　　To a' this place.

167

What was I, or my generation,
That I should get such exaltation?
I, wha deserv'd most just damnation,
   For broken laws
Sax thousand years ere my creation,
   Thro' **Adam**'s cause.

When from my mother's womb I fell,
Thou might hae plunged me deep in hell,
gums To gnash my gooms, & weep, & wail,
   In burning lakes,
Where damned devils roar & yell
   Chain'd to their stakes.

Yet I am here, a chosen sample,
To shew thy grace is great & ample:
I'm here, a pillar o' thy temple
   Strong as a rock,
A guide, a ruler & example
   To a' thy flock.

But yet – O Lord – confess I must –
troubled At times I'm fash'd wi' fleshly lust;
And sometimes too, in warldly trust
   Vile Self gets in;
But thou remembers we are dust,
   Defil'd wi' sin.

last night;
knowest O Lord – yestreen – thou kens – wi' Meg –
Thy pardon I sincerely beg!
O may't ne'er be a living plague,
   To my dishonor!
And I'll ne'er lift a lawless leg
   Again upon her.

Besides, I farther maun avow,
Wi' Leezie's lass, three times – I trow –
But, Lord, that friday I was fou   *drunk*
     When I cam near her;
Or else, thou kens, thy servant true
     Wad never steer her.   *Would; meddle with*

Maybe thou lets this fleshly thorn
Buffet thy servant e'en & morn,
Lest he o'er proud & high should turn,
     That he's sae gifted;
If sae, thy hand maun e'en be borne
     Untill thou lift it.

Lord bless thy Chosen in this place,
For here thou has a chosen race:
But God, confound their stubborn face,
     And blast their name,
Wha bring thy rulers to disgrace
     And open shame.

Lord mind Gaun Hamilton's deserts!
He drinks, & swears, & plays at cartes,   *cards*
Yet has sae mony taking arts
     Wi' Great & Sma',
Frae God's ain priest the people's hearts
     He steals awa.

And when we chasten'd him therefore,
Thou kens how he bred sic a splore,   *disturbance*
And set the warld in a roar
     O' laughin at us:
Curse thou his basket and his store,
     Kail & potatoes.

Lord hear my earnest cry & prayer
Against that Presbytry of Ayr!
Thy strong right hand, Lord, make it bare
   Upon their heads!
do not Lord visit them, & dinna spare,
    For their misdeeds!

O Lord my God, that glib-tongu'd Aiken!
My very heart & flesh are quaking
To think how I sat, sweating, shaking,
   And piss'd wi' dread,
hanging While Auld wi' hingin lip gaed sneaking
    And hid his head!

Lord, in thy day o' vengeance try him!
Lord, visit him that did employ him!
And pass not in thy mercy by them;
   Nor hear their prayer;
But for thy people's sake destroy them,
    And dinna spare!

But Lord; remember me & mine
Wi' mercies temporal & divine!
wealth That I for grace & gear may shine,
   Excell'd by nane!
And a' the glory shall be thine!
    Amen! Amen!

WRITTEN IN A WRAPPER INCLOSING
A LETTER TO CAPT^N GROSE[1],

TO BE LEFT WITH MR CARDONNEL ANTIQUARIAN

Ken ye ought o' Captain Grose? *Know*
      Igo & ago,
If he's amang his friends or foes?
      Iram coram dago.

Is he South, or is he North?
      Igo & ago,
Or drowned in the river Forth?
      Iram coram dago.

Is he slain by Highland bodies? *creatures*
      Igo & ago,
And eaten like a weather-haggis? *wether-*
      Iram coram dago.

Is he to Abram's bosom gane?
      Igo & ago,
Or haudin Sarah by the wame? *holding; waist*
      Iram coram dago.

Whare'er he be, the Lord be near him!
      Igo & ago,
As for the deil, he daur na steer him, *meddle with*
      Iram coram dago.

1. See p. 161. – EDD.

But please transmit th' inclosed letter,
  Igo & ago,
Which will oblidge your humble debtor,
  Iram coram dago.

have old
stones

So may ye hae auld stanes in store,
  Igo & ago,
The very stanes that Adam bore;
  Iram coram dago.

So may ye get in glad possession,
  Igo & ago,
The coins o' Satan's Coronation!
  Iram coram dago.

THE JOLLY BEGGARS

A Cantata

RECITATIVO

When lyart leaves bestrow the yird,   *withered; earth*
Or wavering like the Bauckie-bird,[1]
  Bedim cauld Boreas' blast;
When hailstanes drive wi' bitter skyte,   *lash*
And infant Frosts begin to bite,
  In hoary cranreuch drest;   *rime*
Ae night at e'en a merry core   *company*
  O' randie, gangrel bodies   *lawless, vagrant*
In Poosie-Nansie's held the splore,   *revel*
  To drink their orra dudies: *spare rags*
    Wi' quaffing, and laughing,
      They ranted an' they sang;   *roistered*
    Wi' jumping, an' thumping,
      The vera girdle[2] rang.

First, niest the fire, in auld, red rags,   *next*
Ane sat; weel brac'd wi' mealy bags,   *beggar's meal-bags*
  And knapsack a' in order;
His doxy lay within his arm;
Wi' usquebae an' blankets warm,   *whisky*
  She blinket on her Sodger:
An' ay he gies the tozie drab   *fuddled*
  The tither skelpan kiss,   *smacking*
While she held up her greedy gab,   *mouth*
  Just like an aumous dish: *alms*

1. The old Scotch name for the Bat.
2. Circular iron plate hung over the fire for baking. – EDD.

hawker's

> Ilk smack still did crack still,
>> Just like a cadger's whip;
>> Then staggering, an' swaggering,
>> He roar'a this ditty up –

AIR

TUNE, *Soldiers joy*

I am a Son of Mars who have been in many wars,
And show my cuts and scars wherever I come;

*   *   *   *

RECITATIVO

rafters shook

rats
inmost hole
corner

dear

> He ended; and the kebars sheuk,
>> Aboon the chorus roar;
> While frighted rattons backward leuk,
>> An seek the benmost bore:
> A fairy Fiddler frae the neuk,
>> He skirl'd out, encore,
> But up arose the martial Chuck,
>> An' laid the loud uproar –

AIR

TUNE, *Sodger laddie*

I once was a Maid tho' I cannot tell when,
And still my delight is in proper young men:

*   *   *   *

RECITATIVE

tinker-hussy
cared not;
took

> Poor Merry andrew, in the neuk,
>> Sat guzzling wi' a Tinker-hizzie;
> They mind't na wha the chorus teuk,

Between themsels they were sae busy:
At length wi' drink an' courting dizzy,
He stoiter'd up an' made a face;   staggered
   Then turn'd, an laid a smack on Grizzie,
Syne tun'd his pipes wi' grave grimace.   Then

AIR

TUNE, *Auld Sir Symon*

Sir Wisdom's a fool when he's fou;
   Sir Knave is a fool in a Session,

*   *   *   *

RECITATIVO

Then niest outspak a raucle Carlin,   rough old
                                  woman
Wha ken't fu' weel to cleek the Sterlin;   steal
For mony a pursie she had hooked,
An had in mony a well been douked: ducked
Her Love had been a Highland laddie;
But weary fa' the waefu' woodie!   curse upon;
                                  gallows
Wi' sighs an' sobs she thus began
To wail her braw John Highlandman –   handsome

AIR

TUNE, *O an' ye were dead Gudeman*

A highland lad my Love was born,
The lalland laws he held in scorn: lowland
But he still was faithfu' to his clan,
My gallant, braw John Highlandman.

   Sing hey my braw John Highlandman!
   Sing ho my braw John Highlandman!

The Jolly Beggars

There's not a lad in a' the lan'
Was match for my John Highlandman.

kilt

With his philibeg, an' tartan plaid,
An' guid Claymore down by his side,
The ladies' hearts he did trepan,
My gallant, braw John Highlandman.

We ranged a' from Tweed to Spey,
An' liv'd like lords an' ladies gay:
For a lalland face he feared none,
My gallant, braw John Highlandman.

They banish'd him beyond the sea,
But ere the bud was on the tree,
Adown my cheeks the pearls ran,
Embracing my John Highlandman.

But Och! they catch'd him at the last,
And bound him in a dungeon fast,
My curse upon them every one,
They've hang'd my braw John Highlandman.

And now a Widow I must mourn
The pleasures that will ne'er return;
No comfort but a hearty can,
When I think on John Highlandman.

RECITATIVO

A pigmy Scraper wi' his Fiddle,
markets; toddle
Wha us'd to trystes an' fairs to driddle,
ample
Her strappan limb an' gausy middle,
(He reach'd nae higher)

Had hol'd his heartie like a riddle,
              An' blawn't on fire.   *blown it*

Wi' hand on hainch, and upward e'e,   *haunch*
He croon'd his gamut, one, two, three,
Then in an arioso key,
              The wee Apollo
Set off wi' allegretto glee
              His giga solo –

AIR

TUNE, *Whistle owre the lave o't*

Let me ryke up to dight that tear,
An' go wi' me an' be my dear;
An' then your every care an' fear
    May whistle owre the lave o't.

*   *   *   *

RECITATIVO

Her charms had struck a sturdy Caird   *tinker*
  As weel as poor Gutscraper;
He taks the Fiddler by the beard,
  An' draws a roosty rapier –   *rusty*
He swoor by a' was swearing worth
  To speet him like a Pliver,   *spit; plover*
Unless he would from that time forth
  Relinquish her for ever:

Wi' ghastly e'e poor Tweedledee
  Upon his hunkers bended,   *hams*

An' pray'd for grace wi' ruefu' face,
    An' so the quarrel ended;
But tho' his little heart did grieve,
    When round the Tinkler prest her,
snigger   He feign'd to snirtle in his sleeve
    When thus the Caird address'd her –

AIR

TUNE, *Clout the Cauldron*

My bonie lass, I work in brass,
    A Tinkler is my station;

*   *   *   *

RECITATIVO

The Caird prevail'd – th' unblushing fair
    In his embraces sunk;
Partly wi' Love o'ercome sae sair,
    An' partly she was drunk:
Sir Violino with an air
spirit   That show'd a man o' spunk,
Wish'd unison between the pair,
    An' made the bottle clunk
              To their health that night.

urchin   But hurchin Cupid shot a shaft,
trick   That play'd a Dame a shavie –
The Fiddler rak'd her, fore and aft,
coop   Behint the Chicken cavie:
Her lord, a wight of Homer's[1] craft,

1. Homer is allowed to be the eldest Ballad singer on record.

Tho' limpan wi' the Spavie,   spavin
  He hirpl'd up an' lap like daft,   hobbled;
    An' shor'd them Dainty Davie   leapt like
              O' boot that night.   mad
                       offered
                       into the
                       bargain

He was a care-defying blade,
  As ever Baçchus listed!
Tho' Fortune sair upon him laid,
  His heart she ever miss'd it.
He had no wish but – to be glad,
  Nor want but – when he thristed;
He hated nought but – to be sad,
  An' thus the Muse suggested
          His sang that night.

AIR

TUNE, *For a' that an' a' that*

I am a Bard of no regard,
  Wi' gentle folks an' a' that;

*   *   *   *

RECITATIVO

So sung the Bard, and Nansie's waws   walls
Shook with a thunder of applause
  Re-echo'd from each mouth!
They toom'd their pocks, they pawn'd their   emptied their
    duds,   bags
They scarcely left to coor their fuds,   cover; tails
  To quench their lowan drouth.   burning
                         thirst
Then owre again the jovial thrang   company
  The Poet did request

untie;
choose

To lowse his pack an' wale a sang,
    A ballad o' the best.
      He, rising, rejoicing
        Between his twa Deborahs,
      Looks round him an' found them
        Impatient for the Chorus.

      *   *   *   *

A fig for those by law protected!
    Liberty's a glorious feast!
Courts for Cowards were erected,
    Churches built to please the Priest.

      *   *   *   *

TO DR. BLACKLOCK

ELLISLAND, 21st Oct. 1789.

Wow, but your letter made me vauntie!   proud
And are ye hale, and weel, and cantie?   cheerful
I ken'd it still your wee bit jauntie
      Wad bring ye to:
Lord send you ay as weel's I want ye,
      And then ye'll do.

The ill-thief blaw the Heron[1] south!   Devil
And never drink be near his drouth!   thirst
He tald mysel by word o' mouth,
      He'd tak my letter;
I lippen'd to the chiel in trouth,   trusted; fellow
      And bade nae better.   asked

But aiblins honest Master Heron   perhaps
Had at the time some dainty fair one,
To ware his theologic care on,   spend
      And holy study;
And tired o' sauls to waste his lear on,   souls; learning
      E'en tried the body.

But what d'ye think, my trusty fier,   companion
I'm turn'd a gauger – Peace be here!
Parnassian queens, I fear, I fear,   queans
      Ye'll now disdain me,
And then my fifty pounds a year
      Will little gain me.

---

1. Robert Heron, who was to write a life of Burns (1797).–EDD.

To Dr. Blacklock

Ye glaiket, gleesome, dainty damies, *giddy*
Wha by Castalia's wimplin streamies, *rippling*
Lowp, sing, and lave your pretty limbies, *Leap*
    Ye ken, ye ken,
That strang necessity supreme is
    'Mang sons o' men.

I hae a wife and twa wee laddies,
They maun hae brose and brats o' duddies; *bits of clothes*
Ye ken yoursels my heart right proud is,
    I need na vaunt,
But I'll sned besoms – thraw saugh woodies, *cut; weave willow twigs*
    Before they want.

Lord help me thro' this warld o' care!
I'm weary sick o't late and air! *early*
Not but I hae a richer share
    Than mony ithers;
But why should ae man better fare,
    And a' men brithers!

Come Firm Resolve take thou the van,
Thou stalk o' carl-hemp in man! *male-*
And let us mind, faint heart ne'er wan *remember*
    A lady fair:
Wha does the utmost that he can,
    Will whyles do mair. *sometimes*

But to conclude my silly rhyme,
(I'm scant o' verse, and scant o' time,)
To make a happy fire-side clime
    To weans and wife, *children*
That's the true pathos and sublime
    Of human life.

To Dr. Blacklock

My compliments to sister Beckie;
And eke the same to honest Lucky,
I wat she is a daintie chuckie,   wot; hen
        As e'er tread clay!
And gratefully my gude auld cockie,
        I'm yours for ay.
           ROBERT BURNS.

ADDRESS TO THE TOOTH-ACHE

*(Written by the Author at a time when he was grievously tormented
by that Disorder.)*

My curse on your envenom'd stang, — sting
That shoots my tortur'd gums alang,
An' thro' my lugs gies mony a bang — ears
       Wi' gnawin vengeance;
Tearing my nerves wi' bitter twang,
       Like racking engines.

A' down my beard the slavers trickle,
I cast the wee stools owre the meikle, — big
While round the fire the hav'rels keckle, — half-wits chuckle
       To see me loup; — leap
I curse an' ban, an' wish a heckle — swear; heckling-comb
       Were i' their doup. — backside

Whan fevers burn, or agues freeze us,
Rheumatics gnaw, or colics squeeze us,
Our neebors sympathize, to ease us,
       Wi' pitying moan;
But thou – the hell o' a' diseases,
       They mock our groan.

O' a' the num'rous human dools, — woes
Ill hairsts, daft bargains, cutty-stools, — Bad harvests; foolish; repentance-
Or worthy friends laid i' the mools, — mould
       Sad sight to see!
The tricks o' knaves, or fash o' fools, — annoyance
       Thou bear'st the gree. — first place

Whare'er that place be, priests ca' hell,
Whar a' the tones o' mis'ry's yell,

184

An' plagues in ranked numbers tell
      In deadly raw,   row
Thou, Tooth-ache, surely bear'st the bell
      Aboon them a'!

O! thou grim mischief-makin chiel,   fellow
That gars the notes o' discord squeel,   makes
Till human-kind aft dance a reel
      In gore a shoe thick,
Gie a' the faes o' Scotland's weal   Give; foes
      A towmond's tooth-ache!   twelve-
                              month's

TO WILLIAM CREECH

Auld chuckie Reekie's sair distrest, *mother-hen / Edinburgh*
Down droops her ance weel burnish't crest,
Nae joy her bonie buskit nest *adorned*
    Can yield ava, *at all*
Her darling bird that she lo'es best,
     Willie's awa!

O Willie was a witty wight,
And had o' things an unco' slight; *uncommon*
Auld Reekie ay he keepit tight,
     And trig an' braw: *trim; handsome*
But now they'll busk her like a fright, *dress*
     Willie's awa!

The stiffest o' them a' he bow'd,
The bauldest o' them a' he cow'd; *boldest*
They durst nae mair than he allow'd,
     That was a law:
We've lost a birkie weel worth gowd, *fellow; gold*
     Willie's awa!

Now gawkies, tawpies, gowks and fools, *louts, milk-sops, dupes*
Frae colleges and boarding schools,
May sprout like simmer puddock-stools *summer / toad-*
     In glen or shaw; *wood*
He wha could brush them down to mools *dust*
     Willie's awa!

The brethren o' the Commerce-Chaumer *-chamber*
May mourn their loss wi' doolfu' clamour; *woeful*

186

To William Creech

He was a dictionar and grammar
        Amang them a';
I fear they'll now mak mony a stammer
        Willie's awa!

Nae mair we see his levee door
Philosophers and Poets pour,
And toothy critics by the score
        In bloody raw!   *row*
The adjutant o' a' the core,   *company*
        Willie's awa!

Now worthy Greg'ry's latin face,
Tytler's and Greenfield's modest grace;
M'Kenzie, Stuart, such a brace
        As Rome ne'er saw;
They a' maun meet some ither place,
        Willie's awa!

Poor Burns – e'en Scotch drink canna quicken,
He cheeps like some bewildered chicken,
Scar'd frae its minnie and the cleckin   *mother;*
        brood
        By hoodie-craw!   *carrion-crow*
Grief's gien his heart an unco kickin',
        Willie's awa!

Now ev'ry sour-mou'd girnin blellum,   *-mouthed*
        snarling
        blockhead
And Calvin's fock, are fit to fell him;   *folk; kill*
And self-conceited critic skellum   *rascal*
        His quill may draw;
He wha could brawlie ward their bellum,   *well;*
        assault
        Willie's awa!

To William Creech

rippling

Up wimpling stately Tweed I've sped,
And Eden scenes on chrystal Jed,
And Ettrick banks now roaring red
                    While tempests blaw;
But every joy and pleasure's fled
                    Willie's awa!

May I be slander's common speech;
A text for infamy to preach;

stretched

And lastly, streekit out to bleach
                    In winter snaw;
When I forget thee, Willie Creech,
                    Tho' far awa!

ruffle

May never wicked fortune touzle him!
May never wicked men bamboozle him!

*pate; old as
cheerfully
scratch*

Until a pow as auld's Methusalem
                    He canty claw!
Then to the blessed, New Jerusalem
                    Fleet wing awa!

VERSES

WRITTEN ON THE WINDOW OF THE INN
AT CARRON[1]

We cam na here to view your works   not
   In hopes to be mair wise,
But only, lest we gang to hell,   go
   It may be nae surprise.

But when we tirled at your door,   rattled
   Your porter dought na bear us,   could not
                               admit
So may (should we to hell-yetts come)   -gates
   Your billy Satan sair us.   brother;
                               serve

EPITAPH

ON A WAG IN MAUCHLINE

Lament 'im Mauchline husbands a',
   He aften did assist ye;
For had ye staid whole weeks awa',
   Your wives they ne'er had miss'd ye.

Ye Mauchline bairns, as on ye pass
   To school in bands thegither,   together
O tread ye lightly on his grass,
   Perhaps he was your father.

1. Where the ironworks are. – EDD.

189

ON A SCHOOLMASTER IN
CLEISH PARISH, FIFESHIRE

Here lie Willie Michie's banes,
 O Satan, when ye tak him,
Gie him the schulin of your weans;
 For clever Deils he'll mak 'em!

schooling;
children

ON WILLIAM NICOL

Ye maggots, feed on Nicol's brain,
 For few sic feasts you've gotten;
And fix your claws in Nicol's heart,
 For deel a bit o't's rotten.

devil

THE BOOK-WORMS

Through and through the inspired leaves,
 Ye maggots make your windings;
But, oh! respect his lordship's taste,
 And spare his golden bindings.

TAM THE CHAPMAN

Packman

As Tam the Chapman on a day
Wi' Death forgather'd by the way,

Tam the Chapman

Weel pleas'd, he greets a wight sae famous,
And Death was nae less pleased wi' Thomas,
Wha cheerfully lays down the pack,
And there blaws up a hearty crack; chat
His social, friendly, honest heart
Sae tickled Death, they could na part:
Sae after viewing knives and garters,
Death takes him hame to gie him quarters.

Songs from Johnson's *Scots Musical Museum*
1788 – 1803

I'M O'ER YOUNG TO MARRY YET

I am my mammy's ae bairn,
   Wi' unco folk I weary, Sir,
And lying in a man's bed,
   I'm fley'd it make me irie, Sir.

only child

strange

*afraid;
eerie*

   *I'm o'er young, I'm o'er young,
     I'm o'er young to marry yet;
   I'm o'er young, 'twad be a sin
     To tak me frae my mammy yet.*

Hallowmass is come and gane,
   The nights are lang in winter, Sir;
And you an' I in ae bed,
   In trowth, I dare na venture, Sir.

Fu' loud and shill the frosty wind
   Blaws thro' the leafless timmer, Sir;
But if ye come this gate again,
   I'll aulder be gin simmer, Sir.

shrill

woods

way

*older be by
summer*

McPHERSON'S FAREWELL

Farewell, ye dungeons, dark and strong,
　　The wretch's destinie!
McPherson's time will not be long,
　　On yonder gallows-tree.

Sae rantingly, sae wantonly,
　　Sae dauntingly gae'd he.
He play'd a spring, and danc'd it round,
　　Below the gallows-tree.

went
lively tune

O what is death but parting breath?
　　On many a bloody plain
I've dar'd his face, and in this place
　　I scorn him yet again!

Untie these bands from off my hands,
　　And bring to me my sword;
And there's no a man in all Scotland,
　　But I'll brave him at a word.

trouble

I've liv'd a life of sturt and strife;
　　I die by treacherie:
It burns my heart I must depart
　　And not avenged be.

Now farewell, light, thou sunshine bright,
　　And all beneath the sky!
May coward shame distain his name,
　　The wretch that dares not die!

WHAT WILL I DO GIN MY
HOGGIE DIE

should;

young sheep

What will I do gin my Hoggie die,
   My joy, my pride, my Hoggie,
My only beast, I had nae mae,
   And vow but I was vogie!   *vain*
The lee-lang night we watch'd the fauld,   *live-long; fold*
   Me and my faithfu' doggie;
We heard nought but the roaring linn,   *waterfall*
   Amang the braes sae scroggie.   *covered with scrub*

But the houlet cry'd frae the Castle wa',   *owl*
   The blitter frae the boggie,   *snipe*
The tod reply'd upon the hill   *fox*
   I trembled for my Hoggie.
When day did daw, and cocks did craw,
   The morning it was foggie;
An unco tyke lap o'er the Dyke,   *strange dog; leaped*
   And maist has kill'd my Hoggie.   *almost*

UP IN THE MORNING EARLY

Cauld blaws the wind frae east to west,
    The drift is driving sairly;
Sae loud and shill's I hear the blast,
    I'm sure it's winter fairly.

Up in the morning's no for me,
    Up in the morning early;
When a' the hills are cover'd wi' snaw,
    I'm sure it is winter fairly.

The birds sit chittering in the thorn,
    A' day they fare but sparely;
And lang's the night frae e'en to morn,
    I'm sure it's winter fairly.

sorely

shrill

TO DAUNTON ME

The blude red rose at Yule may blaw,
The simmer-lillies bloom in snaw,
The frost may freeze the deepest sea,
But an auld man shall never daunton me.

To daunton me, and me sae young,
Wi' his fause heart and flatt'ring tongue,
That is the thing you ne'er shall see,
For an auld man shall never daunton me.

For a' his meal and a' his maut,   malt
For a' his fresh beef and his saut,
For a' his gold and white monie,
An auld man shall never daunton me.

His gear may buy him kye and yowes,   money;
                                                          kine; sheep
His gear may buy him glens & knowes,   knolls
But me he shall not buy nor fee,   hire
For an auld man shall never daunton me.

He hirples twa-fauld as he dow,   limps bent
                                                          double; can
Wi' his teethless gab and his auld beld pow,   mouth; bald
                                                          head
And the rain rains down frae his red blear'd e'e,
That auld man shall never daunton me.

O'ER THE WATER TO CHARLIE

Come boat me o'er, come row me o'er,
  Come boat me o'er to Charlie;
I'll gie John Ross another bawbee,
  To boat me o'er to Charlie.

  We'll o'er the water, we'll o'er the sea,
    We'll o'er the water to Charlie;
  Come weal, come woe, we'll gather and go,
    And live or die wi' Charlie.

I lo'e weel my Charlie's name,
  Tho' some there be abhor him:
But O, to see auld Nick gaun hame,
  And Charlie's faes before him!

going
foes

I swear and vow by moon and stars,
  And sun that shines so early!
If I had twenty thousand lives,
  I'd die as aft for Charlie.

RATTLIN, ROARIN WILLIE

O Rattlin, roarin Willie,
  O he held to the fair,
An' for to sell his fiddle
  And buy some other ware;
But parting wi' his fiddle,
  The saut tear blin't his e'e;
And Rattlin, roarin Willie,
  Ye're welcome hame to me.

O Willie, come sell your fiddle,
  O sell your fiddle sae fine;
O Willie, come sell your fiddle,
  And buy a pint o' wine;
If I should sell my fiddle,
  The warl' would think I was mad,
For monie a rantin day   merry
  My fiddle and I hae had.

As I cam by Crochallan,[1]
  I cannily keekit ben,   cautiously
                                           looked in
Rattlin, roarin Willie
  Was sitting at yon boord-en',   head of the
                                           table
Sitting at yon boord-en',
  And amang guid companie;
Rattlin, roarin Willie,
  Ye're welcome hame to me!

1. An Edinburgh club. – EDD.

AY WAUKIN, O

waking

Simmer's a pleasant time,
  Flowers of ev'ry colour;
The water rins o'er the heugh,
  And I long for my true lover!

Ay waukin, O,
  Waukin still and weary:
Sleep I can get nane,
  For thinking on my Dearie.

When I sleep I dream,
  When I wauk I'm irie;
Sleep I can get nane
  For thinking on my Dearie.

Lanely night comes on,
  A' the lave are sleepin:
I think on my bony lad
  And I bleer my een wi' greetin.

(marginal glosses) crag · eerie · rest · weeping

202

MY LOVE SHE'S BUT A LASSIE YET

My love she's but a lassie yet,
My love she's but a lassie yet,
We'll let her stand a year or twa,
She'll no be half sae saucy yet.

I rue the day I sought her O,
I rue the day I sought her O,
Wha gets her needs na say he's woo'd,
But he may say he's bought her O.

Come draw a drap o' the best o't yet,
Come draw a drap o' the best o't yet:
Gae seek for pleasure whare ye will,
But here I never misst it yet.

We're a' dry wi' drinking o't,
We're a' dry wi' drinking o't:
The minister kisst the fidler's wife,
He could na preach for thinkin o't.

MY BONY MARY

Go, fetch to me a pint o' wine,
    And fill it in a silver tassie;
That I may drink before I go
    A service to my bonie lassie.
The boat rocks at the Pier o' Leith,
    Fu' loud the wind blaws frae the Ferry,
The ship rides by the Berwick-law,
    And I maun leave my bony Mary.

The trumpets sound, the banners fly,
    The glittering spears are ranked ready,
The shouts o' war are heard afar,
    The battle closes deep and bloody:
It's not the roar o' sea or shore,
    Wad mak me langer wish to tarry;
Nor shouts o' war that's heard afar,
    It's leaving thee, my bony Mary!

cup

I LOVE MY JEAN

Of a' the airts the wind can blaw,   *directions*
  I dearly like the west,
For there the bony Lassie lives,
  The Lassie I lo'e best:
There's wild-woods grow, and rivers row,   *roll*
  And mony a hill between;
But day and night my fancy's flight
  Is ever wi' my Jean.

I see her in the dewy flowers,
  I see her sweet and fair;
I hear her in the tunefu' birds,
  I hear her charm the air:
There's not a bony flower, that springs
  By fountain, shaw, or green,   *wood*
There's not a bony bird that sings,
  But minds me o' my Jean.

rest of it

First when Maggy was my care,
Heaven, I thought, was in her air;
Now we're married, spier nae mair,
    But Whistle o'er the lave o't.

ask no
more

Meg was meek and Meg was mild,
Sweet and harmless as a child;
Wiser men than me's beguil'd,
    So Whistle o'er the lave o't.

How we live, my Meg and me,
How we love and how we gree;
I carena by how few may see,
    Whistle o'er the lave o't.

Wha I wish were maggots meat,
Dish'd up in her winding-sheet;
I could write – but Meg maun see't,
    Whistle o'er the lave o't.

is sure to

O WERE I ON PARNASSUS HILL

O were I on Parnassus hill;
Or had o' Helicon my fill;
That I might catch poetic skill,
    To sing how dear I love thee.
But Nith maun be my Muses well,
My Muse maun be thy bonie sell;
On Corsincon[1] I'll glowr and spell,   gaze; speak
    And write how dear I love thee.

Then come, sweet Muse, inspire my lay!
For a' the lee-lang simmer's day,   live-long
I couldna sing, I couldna say,
    How much, how dear, I love thee.
I see thee dancing o'er the green,
Thy waist sae jimp, thy limbs sae clean,   slender
Thy tempting lips, thy roguish een –   eyes
    By Heaven and Earth I love thee.

By night, by day, a-field, at hame,
The thoughts o' thee my breast inflame;
And ay I muse and sing thy name,
    I only live to love thee.
Tho' I were doom'd to wander on,
Beyond the sea, beyond the sun,
Till my last, weary sand was run;
    Till then – and then I love thee.

1. See note on p. 241. – EDD.

JOHN ANDERSON MY JO

dear

John Anderson my jo, John,
 When we were first Acquent;
Your locks were like the raven,
 Your bony brow was brent;
But now your brow is beld, John,
 Your locks are like the snaw;
But blessings on your frosty pow,
 John Anderson my Jo.

John Anderson my jo, John,
 We clamb the hill the gither;
And mony a canty day John,
 We've had wi' ane anither:
Now we maun totter down, John,
 And hand in hand we'll go;
And sleep the gither at the foot,
 John Anderson my Jo.

acquainted

smooth

bald

head

together

cheerful

MERRY HAE I BEEN TEETHIN
A HECKLE

flax-comb

O merry hae I been teethin a heckle,
    An' merry hae I been shapin a spoon:
O merry hae I been cloutin a kettle,
    An' kissin my Katie when a' was done.

patching

O, A' the lang day I ca' at my hammer,
    An' a' the lang day I whistle and sing,
O, A' the lang night I cuddle my kimmer,
    An' a' the lang night as happy's a king.

drive

lass

Bitter in dool I lickit my winnins
    O' marrying Bess, to gie her a slave:
Blest be the hour she cool'd in her linnens,
    And blythe be the bird that sings on her grave!

sorrow;
tasted my
reward

winding-
sheet

Come to my arms, my Katie, my Katie,
    An' come to my arms and kiss me again!
Druken or sober here's to thee, Katie!
    And blest be the day I did it again.

THE RANTIN DOG THE DADDIE O'T

rollicking

O wha my babie-clouts will buy,
O Wha will tent me when I cry;
Wha will kiss me where I lie.
    The rantin dog the daddie o't.

O Wha will own he did the faut,
O wha will buy the groanin maut,
O Wha will tell me how to ca't.
    The rantin dog the daddie o't.

When I mount the Creepie-chair,
Wha will sit beside me there,
Gie me Rob, I'll seek nae mair,
    The rantin dog the Daddie o't.

Wha will crack to me my lane;
Wha will mak me fidgin fain;
Wha will kiss me o'er again.
    The rantin dog the Daddie o't.

Marginal glosses:
-clothes
attend to
fault
ale for the nurse
name it
penance-stool
talk; alone
tingling with fondness

WILLIE BREW'D A PECK O' MAUT   malt

O Willie brew'd a peck o' maut,
  And Rob and Allan cam to see;
Three blyther hearts, that lee lang night,   live-long
  Ye wad na found in Christendie.

  We are na fou, We're nae that fou,   drunk
    But just a drappie in our e'e;   drop; eye
  The cock may craw, the day may daw,
    And ay we'll taste the barley bree.   brew

Here are we met, three merry boys,
  Three merry boys I trow are we;
And mony a night we've merry been,
  And mony mae we hope to be!

It is the moon, I ken her horn,
  That's blinkin in the lift sae hie;   sky; high
She shines sae bright to.wyle us hame,   entice
  But by my sooth she'll wait a wee!

Wha first shall rise to gang awa,   go
  A cuckold, coward loun is he!   scamp
Wha first beside his chair shall fa',
  He is the king amang us three!

TAM GLEN

My heart is a breaking, dear Tittie, *[sister]*
   Some counsel unto me come len',
To anger them a' is a pity,
   But what will I do wi' Tam Glen.

I'm thinking, wi' sic a braw fellow, *[handsome]*
   In poortith I might mak a fen: *[poverty; shift]*
What care I in riches to wallow,
   If I mauna marry Tam Glen. *[must not]*

There's Lowrie the laird o' Dumeller,
   'Gude day to you brute' he comes ben: *[in]*
He brags and he blaws o' his siller, *[money]*
   But when will he dance like Tam Glen.

My Minnie does constantly deave me, *[mother; deafen]*
   And bids me beware o' young men;
They flatter, she says, to deceive me,
   But wha can think sae o' Tam Glen.

My Daddie says, gin I'll forsake him, *[if]*
   He'll gie me gude hunder marks ten:
But, if it's ordain'd I maun take him,
   O wha will I get but Tam Glen.

Yestreen at the Valentines' dealing, *[Last night]*
   My heart to my mou gied a sten; *[mouth; leap]*
For thrice I drew ane without failing,
   And thrice it was written, Tam Glen.

Tam Glen

The last Halloween I was waukin
  My droukit sark-sleeve,[1] as ye ken;
His likeness cam up the house staukin,
  And the very grey breeks o' Tam Glen!

Come counsel, dear Tittie, don't tarry;
  I'll gie you my bonie black hen,
Gif ye will advise me to Marry
  The lad I lo'e dearly, Tam Glen.

watching
drenched
shift-

1. See *Halloween*, p. 74. – EDD.

O meikle thinks my Luve o' my beauty,
  And meikle thinks my Luve o' my kin;
But little thinks my Luve, I ken brawlie,
  My tocher's the jewel has charms for him.
It's a' for the apple he'll nourish the tree;
It's a' for the hiney he'll cherish the bee,
My laddie's sae meikle in love wi' the siller,
  He canna hae luve to spare for me.

Your proffer o' luve's an airle-penny,
  My tocher's the bargain ye wad buy;
But an ye be crafty, I am cunnin,
  Sae ye wi' anither your fortune maun try.
Ye're like to the timmer o' yon rotten wood,
  Ye're like to the bark o' yon rotten tree,
Ye'll slip frae me like a knotless thread,
  An' ye'll crack your credit wi' mae nor me.

THE BONNY WEE THING

Bonie wee thing, canie wee thing,   gentle
    Lovely wee thing, was thou mine;
I wad wear thee in my bosom,
    Least my Jewel I should tine.   lose

Wishfully I look and languish
    In that bonie face of thine;
And my heart it stounds wi' anguish   throbs
    Lest my wee thing be na mine.

Wit, and Grace, and Love, and Beauty,
    In ae constellation shine;
To adore thee is my duty,
    Goddess o' this soul o' mine!

AE FOND KISS[1]

Ae fond kiss, and then we sever;
Ae farewell and then for ever!
Deep in heart-wrung tears I'll pledge thee,
Warring sighs and groans I'll wage thee.
Who shall say that fortunes grieves him
While the star of hope she leaves him?
Me, nae chearfu' twinkle lights me;
Dark despair around benights me.

I'll ne'er blame my partial fancy,
Naething could resist my Nancy:
But to see her, was to love her;
Love but her, and love for ever.
Had we never lov'd sae kindly,
Had we never lov'd sae blindly,
Never met – or never parted,
We had ne'er been broken-hearted.

Fare thee weel, thou first and fairest!
Fare thee weel, thou best and dearest!
every   Thine be ilka joy and treasure,
Peace, Enjoyment, Love and Pleasure!
Ae fond kiss, and then we sever;
Ae fareweel, Alas! for ever!
Deep in heart-wrung tears I'll pledge thee,
Warring sighs and groans I'll wage thee.

1. In Johnson this song is entitled 'Rory Dall's Port' after the tune.
–EDD.

THE WEARY PUND O' TOW

pound; yarn

The weary pund, the weary pund,
The weary pund o' tow;
I think my wife will end her life,
Before she spin her tow.

I bought my wife a stane o' lint

stone; flax

   As gude as e'er did grow;
And a' that she has made o' that

   Is ae poor pund o' tow.

one

There sat a bottle in a bole,

hole in the wall

   Beyont the ingle low;

flame

And ay she took the tither souk,

the other suck

   To drouk the stourie tow.

drench the dusty

Quoth I, for shame, ye dirty dame,

   Gae spin your tap o' tow!

bunch

She took the rock, and wi' a knock,

distaff

   She brak it o'er my pow.

head

At last her feet, I sang to see't,

   Gaed foremost o'er the knowe;

went; hill

And or I wad anither jad,

ere; wed; jade

   I'll wallop in a tow.

rope

I HAE A WIFE O' MY AIN

I hae a wife o' my ain,
   I'll partake wi' naebody;
I'll tak Cuckold frae nane,
   I'll gie Cuckold to naebody.

I hae a penny to spend,
   There, thanks to naebody;
I hae naething to lend,
   I'll borrow frae naebody.

I am naebody's lord,
   I'll be slave to naebody;
I hae a gude braid sword,
   I'll tak dunts frae naebody.

knocks

I'll be merry and free,
   I'll be sad for naebody;
Naebody cares for me,
   I care for naebody.

O, FOR ANE AND TWENTY, TAM!

An O, for ane and twenty Tam!
    An hey, sweet ane & twenty, Tam!
I'll learn my kin a rattlin sang,
    An I saw ane and twenty, Tam.

They snool me sair, & haud me down,   snub; sore; hold
    And gar me look like bluntie, Tam;   make; a stupid
But three short years will soon wheel roun',
    And then comes ane & twenty, Tam.

A gleib o' lan', a claut o' gear,   piece; handful of money
    Was left me by my Auntie, Tam;
At kith or kin I need na spier,   Of; ask
    An I saw ane and twenty, Tam.

They'll hae me wed a wealthy coof,   fool
    Tho' I mysel hae plenty, Tam;
But hearst thou, laddie, there's my loof,   hand
    I'm thine at ane and twenty, Tam!

BESS AND HER SPINNING WHEEL

O Leeze me on my spinning-wheel,
And leeze me on my rock and reel;
Frae tap to tae that cleeds me bien,
And haps me fiel and warm at e'en!
I'll set me down and sing and spin,
While laigh descends the simmer sun,
Blest wi' content, and milk and meal,
O leeze me on my spinnin-wheel.

On ilka hand the burnies trot,
And meet below my theekit cot;
The scented birk and hawthorn white
Across the pool their arms unite,
Alike to screen the birdie's nest,
And little fishes caller rest:
The sun blinks kindly in the biel',
Where, blythe I turn my spinnin wheel.

On lofty aiks the cushats wail,
And Echo cons the doolfu' tale;
The lintwhites in the hazel braes,
Delighted, rival ithers lays:
The craik amang the claver hay,
The pairtrick whirrin o'er the ley,
The swallow jinkin round my shiel,
Amuse me at my spinnin wheel.

Wi' sma' to sell, and less to buy,
Aboon distress, below envy,
O wha wad leave this humble state,

Glosses:

Lief is me
distaff
top to toe; clothes; comfortably wraps; well
low

every; brooks
thatched
birch
cool
shelter

oaks; wood pigeons
linnets
each other's
corncraik; clover
partridge; meadow
darting; cot

little
Above

Bess and her Spinning Wheel

For a' the pride of a' the great?
Amid their flairing, idle toys,
Amid their cumbrous, dinsome joys,
Can they the peace and pleasure feel
Of Bessy at her spinnin wheel!

THE BANKS O' DOON

Ye Banks and braes o' bonie Doon,
 How can ye bloom sae fresh and fair;
How can ye chant, ye little birds,
 And I sae weary fu' o' care!
Thou'll break my heart thou warbling bird,
 That wantons thro' the flowering thorn:
Thou minds me o' departed joys,
 Departed never to return.

Oft hae I rov'd by bonie Doon,
 To see the rose and woodbine twine;
every And ilka bird sang o' its luve,
 And fondly sae did I o' mine.
Wi' lightsome heart I pu'd a rose,
 Fu' sweet upon its thorny tree;
stole And my fause luver staw my rose,
 But, ah! he left the thorn wi' me.

SIC A WIFE AS WILLIE HAD

Willie Wastle dwalt on Tweed,
   The spot they ca'd it Linkumdoddie;
Willie was a wabster gude,   *weaver*
   Cou'd stown a clue wi' ony bodie; *have stolen; clew*
He had a wife was dour and din,   *stubborn; dun*
   O Tinkler Maidgie was her mither,
Sic a wife as Willie had
   I wad na gie a button for her.

She has an e'e, she has but ane,
   The cat has twa the very colour;
Five rusty teeth forbye a stump,   *besides*
   A clapper tongue wad deave a miller; *deafen*
A whiskin beard about her mou,
   Her nose and chin they threaten ither; *each other*
Sic a wife as Willie had,
   I wad na gie a button for her.

She's bow-hough'd, she's hem shin'd, *-legged; large shinned*
   Ae limpin leg a hand breed shorter; *One; breadth*
She's twisted right she's twisted left,
   To balance fair in ilka quarter: *each*
She has a hump upon her breast,
   The twin o' that upon her shouther; *shoulder*
Sic a wife as Willie had,
   I wad na gie a button for her.

Sic a Wife as Willie Had

Auld baudrans by the ingle sits, *Old pussie*
    An' wi' her loof her face a washin; *paw*
But Willie's wife is nae sae trig, *trim*
    She dights her grunzie wi' a hushion; *wipes; mouth; stocking-leg*
Her walie nieves like midden-creels, *ample fists; dung-*
    Her face wad fyle the Logan water; *foul*
Sic a wife as Willie had,
    I wad na gie a button for her.

HEY CA' THRO'

carry on

Up wi' the carls of Dysart,
  And the lads o' Buckhiven,
And the Kimmers o' Largo,
  And the lasses o' Leven.

Hey ca' thro' ca' thro'
For we hae mickle a do,
Hey ca' thro' ca' thro'
For we hae mickle a do.

We hae tales to tell,
  And we hae sangs to sing;
We hae pennies to spend,
  And we hae pints to bring.

We'll live a' our days,
  And them that comes behin',
Let them do the like,
  And spend the gear they win.

men

women

much to do

wealth

THE DEIL'S AWA WI' TH'
EXCISEMAN

The deil cam fiddlin thro' the town,
   And danc'd awa wi' th' Exciseman;
every;
Devil And ilka wife cries, auld Mahoun,
   I wish you luck o' the prize, man.

The deil's awa the deil's awa
   The deil's awa wi' th' Exciseman,
He's danc'd awa he's danc'd awa
   He's danc'd awa wi' th' Exciseman.

malt We'll mak our maut and we'll brew our drink,
   We'll laugh, sing, and rejoice, man;
hearty; big And mony braw thanks to the meikle black deil,
   That danc'd awa wi' th' Exciseman.

There's threesome reels, there's foursome reels,
   There's hornpipes and strathspeys, man,
But the ae best dance e'er cam to the Land
   Was, the deil's awa wi' th' Exciseman.

THE LOVELY LASS OF INVERNESS

The lovely lass o' Inverness,
   Nae joy nor pleasure can she see;
For e'en and morn she cries, Alas!
   And ay the saut tear blins her e'e.
Drumossie moor, Drumossie day,   Culloden
   A waefu' day it was to me;   woeful
For there I lost my father dear,
   My father dear and brethren three.

Their winding sheet the bludy clay,
   Their graves are growing green to see;
And by them lies the dearest lad
   That ever blest a woman's e'e!
Now wae to thee thou cruel lord,
   A bludy man I trow thou be;
For mony a heart thou has made sair   sore
   That ne'er did wrang to thine or thee!

A RED, RED ROSE

O my Luve's like a red, red rose,
   That's newly sprung in June.
O my Luve's like the melodie
   That's sweetly play'd in tune.

As fair art thou, my bonie lass,
   So deep in luve am I;
And I will love thee still, my Dear,
   Till a' the seas gang dry.

Till a' the seas gang dry, my Dear,
   And the rocks melt wi' the sun:
I will love thee still, my Dear,
   While the sands o' life shall run:

And fare thee weel, my only Luve!
   And fare thee weel, a while!
And I will come again, my Luve,
   Tho' it ware ten thousand mile!

AULD LANG SYNE

Old long ago

Should auld acquaintance be forgot
  And never brought to mind?
Should auld acquaintance be forgot,
  And auld lang syne!

  For auld lang syne, my jo,
    For auld lang syne,
  We'll tak a ¹cup o' kindness yet
    For auld lang syne.

And surely ye'll be your pint stowp!   stand
  And surely I'll be mine!
And we'll tak a cup o' kindness yet,
  For auld lang syne.

We twa hae run about the braes,
  And pou'd the gowans fine;   pulled
But we've wander'd mony a weary fitt,   foot
  Sin auld lang syne.   Since

We twa hae paidl'd in the burn,   waded
  Frae morning sun till dine;   dinner-time
But seas between us braid hae roar'd,   broad
  Sin auld lang syne.

And there's a hand, my trusty fiere!   companion
  And gie's a hand o' thine!   give me
And we'll tak a right gude-willie-waught, hearty
                                           draught
  For auld lang syne.

  1. Some sing, Kiss, in place of Cup.

229

COMIN THRO' THE RYE

Comin thro' the rye, poor body,
  Comin thro' the rye,
She draigl't a' her petticoatie
  Comin thro' the rye.

Oh Jenny's a' weet, poor body,
  Jenny's seldom dry,
She draigl't a' her petticoatie
  Comin thro' the rye.

Gin a body meet a body
  Comin thro' the rye,
Gin a body kiss a body
  Need a body cry.

Gin a body meet a body
  Comin thro' the glen;
Gin a body kiss a body
  Need the warld ken!

draggled

wet; creature

Should

CHARLIE HE'S MY DARLING

'Twas on a monday morning,
   Right early in the year,
That Charlie came to our town,
   The young Chevalier.

   An' Charlie he's my darling,
   My darling, my darling,
   Charlie he's my darling,
     The young Chevalier.

As he was walking up the street,
   The city for to view,
O there he spied a bonie lass
   The window looking thro'.

Sae light's he jimped up the stair,
   And tirled at the pin;   rattled
And wha sae ready as hersel,
   To let the laddie in.

He set his Jenny on his knee,
   All in his Highland dress;
For brawlie weel he ken'd the way   full well
   To please a bonie lass.

It's up yon hethery mountain,
   And down yon scroggy glen,   covered with scrub
We daur na gang a milking,   daren't go
   For Charlie and his men.

FOR THE SAKE O' SOMEBODY

sore
My heart is sair, I dare na tell,
 My heart is sair for Somebody;
I could wake a winter-night
 For the sake o' Somebody.
  Oh-hon! for Somebody!
  Oh-hey! for Somebody!
I could range the world around
 For the sake o' Somebody.

Ye Powers that smile on virtuous love,
 O, sweetly smile on Somebody!
every
Frae ilka danger keep him free,
 And send me safe my Somebody.
  Oh-hon! for Somebody!
  Oh-hey! for Somebody!
I wad do – what wad I not –
 For the sake o' Somebody!

THE CARDIN O'T

I coft a stane o' haslock woo,
   To make a wat to Johnie o't;
For Johnie is my only jo,
   I lo'e him best of onie yet.

> *The cardin o't, the spinnin o't,*
> *The warpin o't, the winnin o't.*
> *When ilka ell cost me a groat,*
> *The taylor staw the lynin o't.*

For though his locks be lyart gray,
   And though his brow be beld aboon,
Yet I hae seen him on a day
   The pride of a' the parishen.

Glosses (right margin):
- bought; stone; fine wool — outer garment — dear
- every
- stole
- hoary
- bald above
- the whole parish

I'LL AY CA' IN BY YON TOWN

I'll ay ca' in by yon town,
* And by yon garden green, again;*
I'll ay ca' in by yon town,
* And see my bonie Jean again.*

There's nane sall ken, there's nane sall guess,
  What brings me back the gate again,
But she my fairest faithfu' lass,
  And stow'nlins we sall meet again.

She'll wander by the aiken tree,
  When trystin time draws near again;
And when her lovely form I see,
  O haith, she's doubly dear again!

(Margin notes: call; farm-cottages · same way · by stealth · oak · meeting · faith)

BANNOCKS O' BEAR MEAL

Cakes;
barley

Bannocks o' bear meal,
Bannocks o' barley,
Here's to the Highlandman's bannocks o' barley

Wha, in a brulzie, will first cry a parley?   brawl
Never the lads wi' the bannocks o' barley.

Wha, in his wae days, were loyal to Charlie?   woeful
Wha but the lads wi' the bannocks o' barley.

IT WAS A' FOR OUR RIGHTFU' KING

It was a' for our rightfu' king
    We left fair Scotland's strand;
It was a' for our rightfu' king,
    We e'er saw Irish land, my dear,
        We e'er saw Irish land.

Now a' is done that men can do,
    And a' is done in vain:
My Love and Native Land fareweel,
    For I maun cross the main, my dear,
        For I maun cross the main.

He turn'd him right and round about,
    Upon the Irish shore,
gave   And gae his bridle reins a shake,
    With, adieu for evermore, my dear,
        With, adieu for evermore.

The soger frae the wars returns,
    The sailor frae the main,
But I hae parted frae my Love,
    Never to meet again, my dear,
        Never to meet again.

When day is gane, and night is come,
    And a' folk bound to sleep;
I think on him that's far awa,
live-long   The lee-lang night & weep, my dear,
        The lee-lang night & weep.

WEE WILLIE GRAY

Wee Willie Gray, an' his leather wallet;
Peel a willie wand, to be him boots and jacket.   willow
The rose upon the breer will be him trouse an'
    doublet,
The rose upon the breer will be him trouse an'
    doublet.

Wee Willy Gray, and his leather wallet;
Twice a lily-flower will be him sark and cravat;   shirt
Feathers of a flee wad feather up his bonnet,
Feathers of a flee wad feather up his bonnet.

ROBIN SHURE IN HAIRST

Robin shure in hairst,
  I shure wi' him;
Fint a heuk had I,
  Yet I stack by him.

I gaed up to Dunse,
  To warp a wab o' plaiden;
At his daddie's yet,
  Wha met me but Robin.

Was na Robin bauld,
  Tho' I was a cotter,
Play'd me sic a trick,
  And me the Eller's dochter?

Robin promis'd me
  A' my winter vittle;
Fient haet he had but three
  Goos feathers and a whittle.

Song from *Edinburgh Evening Courant*, 1795

THE DUMFRIES VOLUNTEERS

Does haughty Gaul invasion threat,
 Then let the louns bewaure, Sir,   rascals
There's wooden walls upon our seas,
 And volunteers on shore, Sir:
The Nith shall run to Corsincon,[1]
 And Criffell[2] sink in Solway,
Ere we permit a foreign foe
 On British ground to rally.

O let us not, like snarling tykes,   curs
 In wrangling be divided,
Till, slap! come in an unco' loun,   foreign
 And wi' a rung decide it!   cudgel
Be Britain still to Britain true,
 Amang oursels united;
For never but by British hands
 Must British wrongs be righted.

The kettle o' the Kirk and State,
 Perhaps a clout may fail in't,   patch
But de'il a foreign tinkler loun
 Shall ever ca' a nail in't: drive
Our fathers blude the kettle bought,
 And wha wad dare to spoil it,
By Heavens! the sacrilegious dog
 Shall fuel be to boil it!

---

1. A high hill at the source of the Nith.
2. A high hill at the confluence of the Nith with Solway Frith.

The Dumfries Volunteers

The wretch that would a tyrant own,
 And th' wretch, his true-sworn brother,
Who'd set the mob above the throne,
 May they be damn'd together!
Who will not sing, GOD SAVE THE KING,
 Shall hang as high's the steeple;
But while we sing, GOD SAVE THE KING,
 We'll ne'er forget THE PEOPLE.

Songs from Thomson's *Original Airs*
1798–1805

O SAW YE BONIE LESLEY

O saw ye bonie Lesley,
  As she gaed o'er the border?
She's gane, like Alexander,
  To spread her conquests farther.
To see her, is to love her,
  And love but her for ever;
For Nature made her what she is,
  And ne'er made sic anither!

Thou art a queen, fair Lesley,
  Thy subjects we before thee:
Thou art divine, fair Lesley,
  The hearts of men adore thee.
The Deil he cou'dna skaithe thee,   harm
  Or aught that wad belang thee!   would
                                        belong to
He'd look into thy bonie face,
  And say, 'I canna wrang thee.'

The powers aboon will tent thee,   above; guard
  Misfortune sha'na steer thee;   meddle with
Thou'rt like themsels sae lovely,
  That ill they'll ne'er let near thee.
Return again, fair Lesley,
  Return to Caledonie!
That we may brag we hae a lass,
  There's nane again sae bonie.

Last May a braw wooer cam' down the lang glen,
_{sorely;}   And sair wi' his love he did deave me;
_{deafen}
     I said, there was naething I hated like men,
       The deuce gae wi'him to believe me, believe me,
       The deuce gae wi'him, to believe me.

_{eyes} He spak o' the darts in my bonie black een,
       And vow'd for my love he was dying;
     I said he might die when he liked for Jean;
       The Lord forgi'e me for lying, for lying,
       The Lord forgi'e me for lying!

_{farm;} A weel stocked mailin, himsel' for the laird,
_{landlord}
       And marriage aff hand were his proffers:
_{let} I never loot on that I kend it, or car'd,
_{worse}   But thought I might hae waur offers, waur offers,
       But thought I might hae waur offers.

But what wad ye think? in a fortnight or less,
       The de'il tak' his taste to gae near her!
He up the lang loan to my black cousin Bess,
       Guess ye how the jad! I could bear her, could
         bear her,
       Guess ye how the jad! I could bear her.

_{next} But a' the niest week as I petted wi' care,
_{fair}   I gaed to the tryste o' Dalgarnock;
     And wha but my fine fickle lover was there,
_{stared}   I glowr'd as I'd seen a warlock, a warlock,
       I glowr'd as I'd seen a warlock.

Last May a Braw Wooer

But owre my left shouther I ga'e him a blink,   shoulder
   Lest neebours might say I was saucy:
My wooer he caper'd as he'd been in drink,
    And vow'd I was his dear lassie, dear lassie,
    And vow'd I was his dear lassie.

I speir'd for my cousin fu' couthy and sweet,   asked after;
   If she had recover'd her hearing;   amiably
And how her new shoon fit her auld, shachl't feet;   misshapen
    But heavens! how he fell a-swearing, a-swearing,
    But heavens! how he fell a-swearing.

He begged, for gude-sake! I wad be his wife,
   Or else I wad kill him with sorrow:
So e'en to preserve the poor body in life,
    I think I maun wed him – to-morrow, to-morrow,
    I think I maun wed him to-morrow.

O WHISTLE, AND I'LL COME TO YOU,
MY LAD

O whistle, and I'll come to you, my lad,
O whistle, and I'll come to you, my lad;
Tho' father and mother and a' should gae mad,
O whistle, and I'll come to you, my lad.

watch
-gate; ajar
Then

But warily tent, when ye come to court me,
And come na unless the back-yett be a-jee;
Syne up the back-style, and let naebody see,
And come, as ye were na coming to me,
And come, as ye were na coming to me.

At kirk, or at market, whene'er ye meet me,
Gang by me as tho' that ye car'd nae a flie;
But steal me a blink o' your bonie black e'e,
Yet look as ye were na looking at me,
Yet look as ye were na looking at me.

sometimes;
disparage

Ay vow and protest that ye carena for me,
And *whyles* ye may lightly my beauty a wee;
But court nae anither, tho' joking ye be,
For fear that she wyle your fancy frae me,
For fear that she wyle your fancy frae me.

MY NANIE'S AWA'

Now in her green mantle blythe nature arrays,
And listens the lambkins that bleat o'er the braes,
While birds warble welcomes in ilka green shaw; every; wood
But to me its delightless, – my Nanie's awa'.

The snaw-drop and primrose our woodlands adorn,
And violets bathe in the weet of the morn;   dew
They pain my sad bosom, sae sweetly they blaw, blow
They mind me o' Nanie – and Nanie's awa'.

Thou lavrock that starts frae the dews of the lawn,
The shepherd to warn of the grey-breaking dawn,
And thou mellow mavis that hails the night fa',
Give over for pity – my Nanie's awa'.

Come autumn, sae pensive, in yellow and grey,
And soothe me wi' tidings o' Nature's decay;
The dark, dreary winter, and wild-driving snaw,
Alane can delight me – now Nanie's awa'.

THE LEA-RIG

sheltered
field

When o'er the hill the eastern star

folding-;
dear
   Tells bughtin-time is near, my jo;

oxen
And owsen frae the furrowed field

dull
   Return sae dowf and weary O:
Down by the burn, where scented birks
   Wi' dew are hanging clear, my jo,
I'll meet thee on the lea-rig,
   My ain kind dearie O.

darkest

eerie

At mid-night hour, in mirkest glen,
   I'd rove and ne'er be irie O,
If thro' that glen I gaed to thee,
   My ain kind dearie O.
Altho' the night were ne'er sae wild,
   And I were ne'er sae weary O,
I'd meet thee on the lea-rig,
   My ain kind dearie O.

The hunter lo'es the morning sun,
   To rouse the mountain deer, my jo;
At noon the fisher seeks the glen,
   Adown the burn to steer, my jo:
Gi'e me the hour o' gloamin grey,
   It makes my heart sae cheary O,
To meet thee on the lea-rig,
   My ain kind dearie O.

Songs from Currie's Edition, 1800

DUNCAN GRAY

Duncan Gray cam here to woo,
  Ha, ha, the wooing o't,
On blythe yule night when we were fu',   drunk
  Ha, ha, the wooing o't,
Maggie coost her head fu' high,   cast
Look'd asklent and unco skeigh,   askance; very skittish
Gart poor Duncan stand abiegh;   Made; off
  Ha, ha, the wooing o't.

Duncan fleech'd, and Duncan pray'd;   wheedled
  Ha, ha, the wooing o't,
Meg was deaf as Ailsa Craig,[1]
  Ha, ha, the wooing o't,
Duncan sigh'd baith out and in,   both
Grat his een baith bleer't and blin',   Wept; eyes
Spak o' lowpin o'er a linn;   Spoke; leaping; waterfall
  Ha, ha, the wooing o't.

Time and chance are but a tide,
  Ha, ha, the wooing o't,
Slighted love is sair to bide,   hard to endure
  Ha, ha, the wooing o't,
Shall I, like a fool, quoth he,
For a haughty hizzie die?   hussy
She may gae to – France for me!
  Ha, ha, the wooing o't.

1. A well-known rock in the frith of Clyde. – CURRIE.

253

How it comes let doctors tell,
  Ha, ha, the wooing o't,
Meg grew sick – as he grew heal,
  Ha, ha, the wooing o't,
Something in her bosom wrings,
For relief a sigh she brings;
eyes   And O, her een, they spak sic things!
  Ha, ha, the wooing o't.

Duncan was a lad o' grace,
  Ha, ha, the wooing o't,
Maggie's was a piteous case,
  Ha, ha, the wooing o't,
Duncan could na be her death,
smothered Swelling pity smoor'd his wrath;
cheerful; Now they're crouse and canty baith,
merry   Ha, ha, the wooing o't.

MARY MORISON

O Mary, at thy window be,
  It is the wish'd, the trysted hour;   appointed
Those smiles and glances let me see,
  That make the miser's treasure poor:
  How blythly wad I bide the stoure,   endure
                                               the turmoil
A weary slave frae sun to sun;
  Could I the rich reward secure,
The lovely Mary Morison.

Yestreen when to the trembling string,   Last night
  The dance gaed thro' the lighted ha',
To thee my fancy took its wing,
  I sat, but neither heard or saw:
  Tho' this was fair, and that was braw,   fine
And yon the toast of a' the town,   that one
  I sigh'd, and said amang them a',
'Ye are na Mary Morison.'

O Mary, canst thou wreck his peace,
  Wha for thy sake wad gladly die!
Or canst thou break that heart of his,
  Whase only faut is loving thee.   fault
  If love for love thou wilt na gie,
At least be pity to me shown;
  A thought ungentle canna be   cannot
The thought o' Mary Morison.

SCOTS, WHA HAE[1]

Scots, wha hae wi' Wallace bled,
Scots, wham Bruce has aften led;
Welcome to your gory bed,
   Or to victorie.

Now's the day, and now's the hour;
See the front o' battle lour;
See approach proud Edward's power –
   Chains and slaverie!

Wha will be a traitor-knave?
Wha can fill a coward's grave?
Wha sae base as be a slave?
   Let him turn and flee!

Wha for Scotland's king and law
Freedom's sword will strongly draw,
Free-man stand, or Free-man fa',
   Let him follow me!

By oppression's woes and pains!
By your sons in servile chains!
We will drain our dearest veins,
   But they shall be free!

Lay the proud usurpers low!
Tyrants fall in every foe!
Liberty's in every blow!
   Let us do, or die!

1. Title in Currie's edition: *Bruce to his Troops on the eve of the Battle of* BANNOCK-BURN.–EDD.

CA' THE YOWES TO THE KNOWES

Ca' the yowes to the knowes,
Ca' them whare the heather growes,
Ca' them whare the burnie rowes,
   My bonie dearie.

brook runs

Hark, the mavis' evening sang
Sounding Clouden's woods amang;[1]
Then a faulding let us gang,
   My bonie dearie.

a-folding

We'll gae down by Clouden side,
Thro' the hazels spreading wide,
O'er the waves, that sweetly glide
   To the moon sae clearly.

Yonder Clouden's silent towers,
Where at moonshine midnight hours,
O'er the dewy bending flowers,
   Fairies dance sae cheary.

Ghaist nor bogle shalt thou fear;
Thou'rt to love and heaven sae dear,
Nocht of ill may come thee near,
   My bonie dearie.

Fair and lovely as thou art,
Thou hast stown my very heart;
I can die – but canna part,
   My bonie dearie.

stolen

1. The river Clouden, a tributary stream to the Nith. – CURRIE.

CONTENTED WI' LITTLE

Contented wi' little, and cantie wi' mair, *merry; more*
Whene'er I forgather wi' sorrow and care,
I gie them a skelp, as they're creepin alang, *smack*
Wi' a cog o' gude swats, and an auld Scottish sang. *wooden vessel; new ale*

I whyles claw the elbow o' troublesome thought; *sometimes scratch*
But man is a soger, and life is a faught: *fight*
My mirth and gude humour are coin in my pouch,
And my Freedom's my lairdship nae monarch dare
   touch.

A towmond o' trouble, should that be my fa', *twelvemonth; lot*
A night o' gude fellowship sowthers it a': *solders*
When at the blythe end of our journey at last,
Wha the deil ever thinks o' the road he has past.

Blind chance, let her snapper and stoyte on her way; *stumble; stagger*
Be't to me, be't frae me, e'en let the jade gae:
Come ease, or come travail; come pleasure, or pain;
My warst word is – 'Welcome and welcome again!' *worst*

258

FOR A' THAT AND A' THAT

Is there, for honest poverty
  That hangs his head, and a' that;
The coward-slave, we pass him by,
  We dare be poor for a' that!
For a' that, and a' that,
  Our toils obscure, and a' that,
The rank is but the guinea's stamp,
  The man's the gowd for a' that.   gold

What though on hamely fare we dine,
  Wear hoddin grey, and a' that;   coarse grey
Gie fools their silks, and knaves their wine,   woollen
  A man's a man for a' that:
For a' that, and a' that,
  Their tinsel show, and a' that;
The honest man, though e'er sae poor,
  Is king o' men for a' that.

Ye see yon birkie, ca'd a lord,   fellow;
  Wha struts, and stares, and a' that;   called
Though hundreds worship at his word,
  He's but a coof for a' that: fool
For a' that, and a' that,
  His ribband, star, and a' that,
The man of independent mind,
  He looks and laughs at a' that.

A prince can mak a belted knight,
  A marquis, duke, and a' that;
But an honest man's aboon his might,   above
  Gude faith he mauna fa' that!   must not try

For A' That and A' That

For a' that, and a' that,
    Their dignities, and a' that,
The pith o' sense, and pride o' worth,
    Are higher ranks than a' that.

Then let us pray that come it may,
    As come it will for a' that,
That sense and worth, o'er a' the earth,
    May bear the gree, and a' that.

*have the
first place*

For a' that, and a' that,
    Its comin yet for a' that,
That man to man, the warld o'er,
    Shall brothers be for a' that.

OH WERT THOU IN THE CAULD BLAST

cold

Oh wert thou in the cauld blast,
  On yonder lea, on yonder lea;
My plaidie to the angry airt,   quarter
  I'd shelter thee, I'd shelter thee:
Or did misfortune's bitter storms
  Around thee blaw, around thee blaw,   blow
Thy bield should be my bosom,   shelter
  To share it a', to share it a'.

Or were I in the wildest waste,
  Sae black and bare, sae black and bare,
The desart were a paradise,
  If thou wert there, if thou wert there.
Or were I monarch o' the globe,
  Wi' thee to reign, wi' thee to reign;
The brightest jewel in my crown,
  Wad be my queen, wad be my queen.

Songs in Cromek's *Reliques*, 1808

YE FLOWERY BANKS

Ye flowery banks o' bonie Doon,
　　How can ye blume sae fair;
How can ye chant, ye little birds,
　　And I sae fu' o' care!

Thou'll break my heart thou bonie bird
　　That sings upon the bough;
Thou minds me o' the happy days　　　reminds
　　When my fause luve was true.

Thou'll break my heart, thou bonie bird
　　That sings beside thy mate;
For sae I sat, and sae I sang,
　　And wist na o' my fate.

Aft hae I rov'd by bonie Doon,
　　To see the wood-bine twine,
And ilka bird sang o' its love,　　　every
　　And sae did I o' mine.

Wi' lightsome heart I pu'd a rose
　　Frae aff its thorny tree,　　　From off
And my fause luver staw the rose,　　　stole
　　But left the thorn wi' me.

THERE WAS A LAD

There was a lad was born in Kyle,[1]
But what na day o' what na style
I doubt its hardly worth the while
    To be sae nice wi' Robin.

Robin was a rovin' Boy,
    Rantin' rovin', rantin' rovin';
Robin was a rovin' Boy,
    Rantin' rovin' Robin.

Our monarch's hindmost year but ane
Was five and twenty days begun,
'Twas then a blast o' Janwar Win'
    Blew hansel in on Robin.

The gossip keckit in his loof,
Quo' scho wha lives will see the proof,
This waly boy will be nae coof,
    I think we'll ca' him Robin.

He'll hae misfortunes great and sma',
But ay a heart aboon them a';
He'll be a credit 'till us a',
    We'll a' be proud o' Robin.

But sure as three times three mak nine,
I see by ilka score and line,
This chap will dearly like our kin',
    So leeze me on thee Robin.

Margin glosses:
which day
Roystering
January / wind
first gift
peered; palm
Quoth she
fine; fool
call
above
to
every
kind
my blessings

1. The district of Ayrshire containing Alloway. —EDD.

266

There was a Lad

Gude faith quo' scho I doubt you Sir,
Ye gar the lasses lie aspar;   make; aspread
But twenty fauts ye may hae waur,   faults; worse
   So blessin's on thee, Robin!

INDEX OF TITLES AND FIRST LINES